D0392490

The Frog Princess of Pelham

Also by Ellen Conford:

Get the Picture, Jenny Archer?
Can Do, Jenny Archer
A Case for Jenny Archer
Jenny Archer, Author
Jenny Archer to the Rescue
A Job for Jenny Archer
Nibble, Nibble, Jenny Archer
What's Cooking, Jenny Archer?
Dear Mom, Get Me Out of Here!
I Love You, I Hate You, Get Lost!

The Frog Princess of Pelham

by Ellen Conford

Little, Brown and Company
BOSTON NEW YORK TORONTO LONDON

First edition

The characters and events in this book are fictitious. Any similarity to real persons, living or dead, is coincidental and not intended by the author.

Library of Congress Cataloging-in-Publication Data
Conford, Ellen.
The frog princess of Pelham / Ellen Conford.—1st ed.
p. cm.
Summary: When a kiss from Danny turns Chandler, a wealthy but lonely orphan, into a frog, Danny's humorous attempts to change her back into a human land the pair on a television talk show.
ISBN 0-316-15246-3
[1. Orphans—Fiction. 2. Frogs—Fiction. 3. Humorous stories.] I. Title.
PZ7.C7593Fr 1997
[Fic]—dc20 96-25046

10 9 8 7 6 5 4 3 2 1

MV-NY

Published simultaneously in Canada by Little, Brown & Company (Canada) Limited

Printed in the United States of America

For Michael and Gloria,
the newlyweds

ONE

Once upon a time . . .

No. "Once upon a time" is for fairy tales, and this is no fairy tale.

A long time ago, in a galaxy far, far away . . .

No. This didn't happen a long time ago, and I've never even been to a nearby galaxy.

A funny thing happened on my way to . . .

No. It wasn't funny. It definitely wasn't funny.

"How I Spent My Winter Vacation"

That's it.

"Survival camp?" I looked up from my beef bouillon and stared at my cousin, Horace. "Are you kidding?"

"No, Chandler, I'm not kidding. I think it would be very good for you."

"So do I," said Felice. Felice is Horace's girlfriend. They've been going together for three years. I think the only reason they haven't married yet is because Horace's last name is Fleer. The thought of being Felice Fleer would make anyone think twice about marriage.

She speared a crouton with two blood-red fingernails and popped it into her mouth. "Besides," she added, "we'll be in Switzerland. You can't stay here by yourself."

"Mrs. Gruen—" I began. Mrs. Gruen is the housekeeper.

"Mrs. Gruen won't be here," Horace reminded me. "Mrs. Gruen will be taking her vacation."

"Of course, you could come to Switzerland with us," Felice said. The look of alarm on Horace's face was almost comical. But he needn't have panicked. There was no sincerity in Felice's invitation. She knew I didn't want to be with them any more than they wanted to be with me. "But you never seem interested in traveling with us." She almost managed a dejected sigh.

"Horace, this is crazy." I put down my spoon. My appetite was gone. "I don't even like camp in the summer. And you're sending me to Idaho, in the mountains, in *February?* Did you ever see the movie *Alive?* Did you ever hear of the Donner Party? They should call it anti-survival camp!"

"Don't be absurd." Horace touched his napkin to his lips. He pushed his soup plate away. Mrs. Gruen brought in a platter of something. I didn't see what it was. I didn't care.

"Why couldn't I go to survival camp in Hawaii, for Pete's sake? At least there I'd have a chance to actually survive." A nasty thought wormed its way into my head. "Or don't you want me to survive?"

"Really, Chandler," scolded Felice. "What a terrible thing to say."

My parents were killed in an auto accident when I was nine. Horace, my only living relative, was appointed my guardian.

Horace is a distant cousin. Most of the time he stays as distant from me as possible. But he keeps in very close touch with my inheritance.

My parents had had a lot of money. In three years I'd have a lot of money. But until my eighteenth birthday, Horace held all the bankbooks.

I stood up and shoved my chair back. "I'm not going," I said.

"You are going," Horace said firmly. "Your plane leaves at nine A.M. Saturday."

"It'll leave without me!"

"No it won't. I've already paid the first half of the fee. It's nonrefundable."

"It's my money!" I shouted. "You're using my money to send me off to freeze in the mountains!"

"I am in charge of your money." As if I needed a reminder. "And I'm doing what I think is best for you. You will make new friends, you will learn survival skills. You may even learn a little something about self-reliance."

"Where will I learn how to survive *you?*" I burst into tears and ran out of the dining room.

I didn't come out of my room until the next morning. I'd spent most of the night trying to figure out how to play hookey from survival camp. In the little snatches of sleep I did get, I dreamed I was clawing my way up the side of an ice-glazed mountain. I kept waking up just after I lost my foothold, and just before I plummeted to my death.

I hoped I had no gift for prophecy. Because short of chaining myself to a major appliance, I could not think of a way to get out of going to Idaho. For that matter, I could hardly force myself to get out of bed.

But today was the last day of school before midwinter break. It might be the last chance I'd get to see my friends. Ever.

I got dressed and went downstairs. No one was in the dining room. Mrs. Gruen looked up from the newspaper as I came into the kitchen.

"What would you like for breakfast?" she asked.

"I'm not hungry."

"Come on, Chandler." Her voice was uncharacteristically sweet. "You must be hungry. You ate so little last night."

"I ate nothing last night," I corrected her. "Except for two spoonfuls of soup."

Why was she suddenly showing such concern? She always kept me well fed and made sure I had clean clothes and clean sheets, but she'd never even tried to fake any tender feelings for me.

I got a pitcher of orange juice from the refrigerator and poured myself a glass. I stuck a piece of bread in the toaster.

She must know what it's like in Idaho in February, I thought. It's got to be pretty bad if even Mrs. Gruen feels sorry for me.

"Is my cousin up yet?" I didn't want to see him. I popped the toast and bit into a dry edge.

"They've both left for the city," Mrs. Gruen said. "They'll pack and go to the airport from there."

Horace has a condo in New York. That's where he spends most of his time.

I put down the toast. "They're flying out tonight, right?"

She nodded.

And I wasn't scheduled to leave till tomorrow morning. If Horace wasn't here, how could he force me to go to camp? He couldn't drag me to the airport. He couldn't stand guard over me till I boarded the plane to Idaho.

For a moment—just a moment—a tiny ray of hope glimmered. I pictured myself *not* falling off a mountain in Idaho. I pictured myself here, in my house, reading, watching videos, and ordering in.

And then I realized that even though Horace wouldn't be around to make sure I got off to Idaho, Mrs. Gruen would.

I threw the toast into the sink and dumped the remains of my orange juice on top of it. I started out of the kitchen.

"Chandler, I wanted to ask you a favor," Mrs. Gruen said.

Aha! That explained it. Mrs. Gruen hadn't suddenly discovered her maternal instinct. She didn't feel sorry for me. She just wanted something. It must be some favor, I thought, to inspire a performance like this.

"Mr. Fleer wants me to take you to the airport tomorrow," she began. "Before I leave for my sister's in Wichita."

"I didn't know that," I said. "I mean, I knew you were going to Wichita, but I didn't know you were taking me to the airport. I didn't even know I was going away until last night."

"Neither did I," she said. "I expected you to go to Switzerland with your cousin."

I don't know how she could have expected that. I never went anywhere with Horace and Felice if I could help it.

"Well, anyhow, I have a supersaver ticket to Wichita," she went on, "but it's for three this afternoon."

That little ray of light started flickering again. If Mrs. Gruen left today, and my flight wasn't till tomorrow . . .

"No problem!" I said. "I can stay by myself one night. Or sleep over at a friend's house. Don't change your plans on my account."

"Oh, bless you, Chandler." She beamed. "They wouldn't let me exchange the ticket, and it would have cost me an extra—"

"Say no more," I cut in.

"Well, there is just one little thing." She leaned forward

and almost whispered it, as if Horace's spies might be lurking in the pantry. "Mr. Fleer might be a little annoyed if he knew I left you a day early—"

"He'll never know the difference," I said. "I certainly won't tell him. You just have a nice visit with your sister, and don't worry about me."

What a break!

I was so lighthearted when she dropped me off at school that I was thinking up new lyrics for show tunes and singing them in my head.

"The world is alive . . . and so is Chandler . . ."

"Doe, a deer, in Idaho, Fa, I will not go so fa . . ."

Well, I didn't say they were good lyrics.

But my mood was good. Until Mason and Jason Gorman spotted me.

"Hey, Princess," Mason said. "You're looking less stuck-up than usual."

"Yeah," said Jason. "Look at her. She's smiling." He stuck his face in front of mine. "I didn't know you smiled at peasants, Princess."

"I'm not smiling at you." I backed away from him, my mood shattering like a smashed window. Why couldn't they leave me alone? What did I ever do to them?

I hardly ever spoke to them. But I hardly ever spoke to anyone, except Lauren and Kelly. I'm just not what you call a smooth talker. I can't make witty conversation with people I don't know very well. So even if I think of something clever, I'm usually too nervous to say it. And sometimes I just blurt out the first thing that pops into my head. So I end up sounding either dumb or sarcastic.

"Oh, shut up," I muttered. (See? Dumb.) I hurried up the front steps to the school's main entrance. *Loathsome little toads.*

Kelly once suggested that maybe they tormented me because they liked me. Lauren thought it was probably because there are some people who simply enjoy tormenting.

My feeling was that they were immature idiots, twins who'd been born with a single brain between them. Without the mental resources to fight a battle of wits one-on-one, they collaborated on making my life miserable.

I was such an easy target.

By lunchtime I was feeling cheerful again. I'd spent most of the morning planning my vacation. What videos would I rent? What books did I want to read? What kind of food should I order in?

I might even go into the city and see some plays. The possibilities were endless. Kelly and Lauren would be away. Lauren was going to visit her grandparents in Florida, and Kelly would be staying with her father in Los Angeles. But I'd been used to entertaining myself for a long time now. And if I wanted, I could talk to them every night on the phone.

It was a beautiful afternoon, warm enough to go outside after lunch without our jackets.

Lauren, Kelly, and I settled near the football field. Kelly rolled up her sleeves. "I'm going to get a head start on my tan," she announced.

"Don't you know how dangerous it is to get a sunburn?" Lauren said.

"I'm not going to get a sun*burn*," Kelly said. "I'm going to get a sun*tan*. I'll come back from L.A. a luscious golden brown. You'll be insanely jealous."

"No I won't," Lauren said. "And I'll live longer."

"Yeah, but palely," Kelly shot back. "On carrot sticks and sprouts. In a dim house with thirty-nine cats."

Lauren is a vegetarian and very concerned about endangered species. Actually, she's concerned about unendangered species too. Kelly accuses her of liking animals better than people. I don't know if that's true, but Lauren certainly has a soft heart.

Sometimes I thought the two of them felt sorry for me because I'm an orphan. Then sometimes I suspected that they hung out with me because they like my pool. But they'd been my closest—my only—friends since sixth grade. If it was because they liked to swim, I told myself I didn't care. It was good to have someone to talk to. Even if I never said much.

"So, what are you going to do over the vacation?" Kelly asked me.

"Horace signed me up for survival camp," I said. "In Idaho. But—"

"Survival camp?" Kelly looked stunned. "Where they leave you in the woods for a week and you try not to die?"

"Right. Except this one's in the mountains."

"Why?" Lauren asked.

"Horace thought it would teach me self-reliance."

Lauren snorted. "How much more self-reliance do you need to learn? You're on your own most of the time as it is."

"I guess he wants me to learn how to be self-reliant without electricity," I said.

"What a gruesome thought." Kelly leaned back on her elbows and held her face up to the sun. "How will you do your hair?"

"But the thing is—" I was about to explain my escape plan when I heard a boy's voice behind me.

"Chandler?"

I looked around. Danny Malone was standing over me.

"Can I see you a minute?" he asked.

"You're seeing me." I didn't sound very gracious, but I was too surprised. I couldn't imagine what Danny would want with me.

"I mean—uh—alone."

"Whoaa!" Kelly turned over on her stomach and leered at me. "Here's an interesting development."

"Kelly!" My face was burning. She couldn't know how I felt about Danny. Nobody knew. I've always thought it was safer to keep my feelings to myself. The less people know about what bothers you, the less they can hurt you.

Danny's face looked a little flushed. Maybe he'd been working on a tan himself. He couldn't be blushing. He wasn't the blushing type.

"What did I say?" Kelly asked innocently.

"Don't be such a child," Lauren scolded. She grabbed Kelly by the arm and hauled her to her feet. "We were just leaving. Weren't we, Kelly?"

"Hey!" Kelly pulled her arm away. "Don't bruise the tan. It hasn't set yet." But she followed Lauren across the grass toward the main entrance, only turning back once to give us a sly grin.

"Well, here we are," I said. "Alone. What do you want?"

I felt like kicking myself. Why did I have to sound so prickly? If I were Danny, I wouldn't want to be alone with me. My face felt hot enough to grill burgers.

Danny looked around. "We're not that alone."

He was right. There were lots of kids lounging in the sun or clustered in groups, talking, throwing Frisbees, munching candy bars. But no one was looking at us, except Mason and Jason Gorman. They weren't close enough to hear whatever it was Danny wanted to tell me, though they'd probably find a way to taunt me about it later.

"Okay, where do you want to go, then?" I asked. My heart started racing. I felt a little shiver run through me. Up until now Danny had never said anything more to me than "Got a pen?"

I let myself imagine for a moment that he was going to say something like "You know, Chan, I've always liked you but I was afraid to tell you."

I dismissed the thought almost as fast as it surfaced. Danny wouldn't be afraid to tell any girl how he felt. He was cute and self-confident and popular—and so were all the girls he'd ever spent time with.

I was ordinary-looking, insecure, and tongue-tied. If he'd wanted to talk to Kelly, for instance, I wouldn't have been surprised.

That must be it, I thought. It's Kelly he's interested in. Maybe he wants me to find out if she likes him.

He led me behind the bleachers. The lacrosse team was practicing on the field, but we were well hidden from them, and they were making a lot of noise anyway.

I couldn't stand the suspense another second. "What is it?" I asked. "What do you want?"

He gave me a shy little grin. "I want to kiss you."

I thought I was going to faint. "You want—me—k-kiss—why?" All I could do was stammer. And turn even redder.

"Can I?"

This can't be happening, I thought. Danny Malone likes

me? The boy I'd dreamed about since October? The boy who could have any girl in school?

"Can I?" he asked again.

"Well—uh—yeah." I didn't sound nearly as willing as I felt, but I was lucky I could say anything. I was trembling and shivering and my heart was pounding. I hoped my lips weren't wet and sloppy, I hoped his lips wouldn't be wet and sloppy. All I could do was gulp a few times, close my eyes, and wait.

His cool, dry lips met mine.

A weird feeling whooshed through me, as if I were tumbling into a deep hole. My body seemed to shrink in on itself as I plunged, faster and faster downward.

Is this how it's supposed to feel when you're kissed? I wondered. I tried not to shriek. Danny would probably be insulted if his kiss made me scream.

But then I did hear a scream, and I didn't know whether it came from me or not, because I couldn't feel my mouth open. But it was nearby, and I was sure Danny wouldn't scream after he kissed me, even if he hadn't enjoyed it very much.

When I opened my eyes, all I could see was an enormous Reebok.

TWO

"Chandler! Where are you?"

It was Danny's voice. But I couldn't see him. I couldn't see anything, except that sneaker, and a lot of green stuff.

"I'm right here," I said. Why was my voice so strange? It sounded like gravel rattling in a pie tin.

"Where?" he demanded. "I don't see you."

"I can't see you either," I said shakily. "All I can see is a sneaker. Where's the rest of you?"

"Right where I was!" he insisted. "But you aren't. Where are you hiding? And why are you talking funny?"

I saw the sneaker turn, and then something white and large with ridges loomed over me.

It was the sole of Danny's Reebok.

"Don't move!" I screamed. The sneaker froze just above my head, then slowly pulled back.

And finally I realized what had happened.

"You shrank me!" I gasped. "That's why I'm down here!"

"Down where?" Danny's head appeared in my line of vision. "Oh, come on, Chandler. Wherever you are. Quit goofing around. I didn't shrink you. People only shrink in movies."

"I'm not goofing around!" I remembered the sensation of falling, and how my body seemed to grow smaller and smaller. "And you're looking right at me! I see your face. You've got a huge zit right between your eyebrows!"

Whatever had happened to me had not improved my social skills.

"Okay, look, I'm not playing this game anymore." He sounded irritated. "'Cause if I'm looking right at you, you're invisible."

"Invisible!" I wailed. "I don't want to be invisible! That's even worse than being shrunk."

"Invisible, shrunk, whatever," he said. "The only thing near me is a frog."

"A frog?" I tried to turn my head, but it didn't turn. My sight didn't seem affected. In fact, my eyes felt very large, and my range of vision much wider than normal. I could see sideways, even though I couldn't turn my head. "I don't see any frog."

Distantly I heard the bell signal the end of lunch period.

Danny's face disappeared. I saw his sneakers start to move away from me.

"Danny, don't go!" I begged. "Don't leave me here!"

He didn't even turn around.

Desperately I tried to run after him. And suddenly I was flying through the air like I'd sprung off a trampoline.

I shrieked again, terrified. The next thing I knew, I was hanging on to his belt, my legs dangling.

"Oh, for Pete's sake." He reached around and plucked me off his belt. He put his face close to mine. His nostrils looked huge. "You can't go into school, frog," he said. "You might get dissected."

"*Frog?*" I croaked. *"I'm a frog?"*

"Chand—?" His eyes turned up in his head. The next thing I knew, we were both on the ground. Only this time the toes of his sneakers were pointing toward the sky.

"Danny! Danny, get up! Are you all right?" I jumped onto his chest. I could feel it rise and fall, feel the beating of his heart. What should I do? I thought frantically. Should I try to give him mouth-to-mouth resuscitation? Was it even possible in my condition?

And then I thought, why am I worrying about him? In a few minutes he'll be conscious again. But I'll still be a *frog*.

"Wake up!" I began hopping on his chest. "Wake up, wake up, wake up!" I was getting hysterical. I heard my own wild, coarse shrieks. I was out of control, for the first time since my parents' death.

Danny's eyelids fluttered. He let out a little moan and started to sit up. I jumped onto his knee.

"What happened?" He rubbed the back of his head.

"You fainted."

He looked down at me. "Oh, my God. I didn't imagine it. You're still here."

"Of course I'm still here! Where am I supposed to go?"

"I have to get to class," he said, sounding dazed. "I have a biology test."

"A test!" I yelled. "Are you crazy? You turned me into a frog. How can you think of a stupid test at a time like this?"

"I didn't turn you into a frog," he said. "How could I do that?"

"You kissed me," I reminded him. "Before you kissed me, I was a person. Now I'm a frog. I think it's pretty obvious."

"That's crazy," he said. "I couldn't have done that. You must have done it to yourself."

"Oh, that's very nice!" I snapped. "Blame the victim. Did I ask you to kiss me?"

"Geez." He put his hand over his eyes. "It was just a stupid bet."

"What?"

He sighed. "Mason Gorman bet me a dollar I couldn't get you to kiss me."

"You kissed me on a bet?" I jumped toward his face and landed on his Adam's apple. "You didn't really want to kiss me?" Maybe later I'd have time to feel insulted, but at the moment there were more urgent things to worry about.

He pulled me off his Adam's apple and put me down on the grass. "Mason said you were the most stuck-up girl in school, so you'd be the hardest—"

"Stuck-up? I'm not stuck-up, you idiot! I'm shy!"

"I guessed that," he said. "But Mason didn't. So I figured it was an easy buck."

I jumped onto his shoulder. "*You turned me into a frog,*" I screamed, "*to win a dollar bet?*"

His shoulder slumped. I clung to his shirt so I wouldn't fall off. "I'm sorry," he said. "But be fair, Chandler. How could I know you'd turn into a frog?"

"Well, I *did*," I said. "Now, what are you going to do about it?"

"What can I do about it?" he asked. "I don't know how to turn a frog into a person."

"Yeah, right. You only know how to turn a person into a frog. Hey!" I jumped down to his arm. "Hey, maybe that's it!"

"What's it?"

"Kiss me again. Maybe I'll change back."

"Kiss you again?" he repeated. He looked at me. It was not a look of love. "Like, now?"

"You're not in the mood?" I said sarcastically. "You want me to woo you with a romantic candlelight dinner of flies and slugs?"

His Adam's apple bobbed. He looked like he was going to pass out again.

"On the lips?" he asked weakly.

"Do I have lips?"

He held me up to his face. *His* lips looked huge. "I'm not sure," he said.

"It doesn't matter," I said. "Just do it."

He took a deep breath. He started to bring me toward his face, then stopped, and held me away. "You feel sort of—um—slimy."

"Well, *excuse* me! Who made me slimy?" And to think, mere moments ago, before he kissed me, I'd been worried about wet lips.

He brought me toward his face again. And faltered again. "No tongues, okay?"

"Don't be disgusting!"

He closed his eyes. I tried to close mine, but they wouldn't close. A sort of film came over them though, making things look a little blurry.

He held me next to his mouth and fleetingly touched my lips (if I had any) to his. It was the shortest kiss in the history of kissing.

My eyes cleared.

I was still in his hand.

He gave an apologetic little shrug. "It wasn't exactly magic, was it?"

"No," I said coldly. "Not in any sense of the word."

THREE

"Well, home sweet home," Danny announced.

From my perch on his shoulder I could see the brass nameplate on the apartment door. *J. Malone. D. Malone.* I heard barking inside.

"You have a dog?" I asked nervously.

"Yeah. You're not afraid of dogs, are you?"

"I have a feeling I'm afraid of anything bigger than a goldfish," I said.

I'd convinced Danny that turning me back into myself was more important than his biology test. And that cutting school for the afternoon would have less impact on his college prospects than being a frog would have on mine.

He opened the door, and a huge, hairy mass flung itself at us. "Woof!"

"Yikes!" I jumped for Danny's head, but I wasn't good

at judging distances yet. I sailed right over him and landed on the edge of an umbrella stand.

The dog charged toward me, woofing hysterically. I jumped off the umbrella stand and landed on a bookcase. The dog wheeled around and bounded for the bookcase.

"No, Bobo!" Danny shouted. "Sit!"

Bobo's whole body wriggled for a moment, then he squatted halfway down, his hindquarters not touching the floor.

"He's only pretending to sit!" I said.

Bobo leaped toward me. "Get him away!" I jumped again, blindly, with no idea where I would land. I found myself on a white counter next to a large glass and metal thing. It had buttons on it. Underneath each button a word was stamped. "Liquefy." "Puree." "Frappé." "Blend."

"Ack! A blender!" I recalled the disgusting joke from my childhood and jumped again. I landed in the sink, on top of a pile of dirty dishes.

My heart was beating so fast, I began to wonder if frogs could have heart attacks.

"Chandler, if you'd stop jumping around he'd calm down," Danny said.

"If I stop jumping around he'll eat me!"

"He won't eat you," Danny said. "He's a sheepdog. He probably just wants to herd you."

But he grabbed Bobo by the collar. "I'll put him in my dad's room," he said. "Until he gets used to you."

"Thank you." I heard Bobo's toenails dragging along the floor, and then a door closing. Danny came back into the kitchen, and I hopped out of the sink back onto the counter.

"Don't you ever clean up?" I asked. "I think I've got jelly on my foot."

"Which foot?" he asked.

"Oh, God. I have four, don't I?"

"Well," he said, "the front two are sort of like little claws."

"I have *claws?*"

"Not really claws," he said. "Practically fingers. They're just a little—um—thin. And pointy. And green. Can't you see them?"

"No," I said miserably.

"Why did you puff yourself up like that?" he asked.

"What do you mean?"

"When Bobo chased you. Your whole body swelled up."

"Great," I croaked. "It's not bad enough being a frog. I have to be a fat frog."

"You're not fat now," he said. "You un-swelled. How do you do that?"

"How should I know? I didn't even know I was doing it. Maybe it's an instinct thing. Like avoiding blenders."

He sat down on a chair and stared at me. "Well," he said finally. "What do we do now?"

I knew what I was going to do.

My throat tightened up. I began to whimper. Danny eyed me curiously till I burst into full-fledged sobs.

"What are you doing?" he asked.

"I'm crying, you dummy! What do you think I'm doing?"

"It sounds more like laughing," he said. He peered at my face. "I don't see any tears."

"I'm crying on the inside," I said.

He cleared his throat. I think he was embarrassed.

"What's the matter?" I snapped. "Haven't you ever seen a frog cry before?"

"Well," he said lamely, "at least you've still got your sense of humor."

"That wasn't humor! That was sarcasm. Can't you tell the difference?"

"Actually, no," he said. "Your voice sounds the same, no matter what you're saying. Except when you scream. And your mouth doesn't open."

"It doesn't?" I was surprised.

"No. How can you talk without opening your mouth?"

"I don't know!" I said. "Why do you keep asking me all these stupid questions? I don't know the first thing about frogs. If I'd known I was going to turn into one, I would have boned up."

He shook his head. "Me neither. All I remember from fourth grade is that you eat flies and need to be near a source of water."

"Water's no problem," I said, "if you'll get the garbage out of the sink. And I won't even discuss the fly-eating issue."

I jumped onto the table and fixed him with a steady stare. (Which was not hard, since I didn't seem to blink.) "I don't want to learn about frogs," I said. "What we need to focus on here is how to turn me back into a human."

He cleared his throat again. "Listen," he began, looking very uncomfortable, "I want you to turn back into a girl again as much as you do—"

"As much as I do?" I said. "I hardly think so."

"Okay, okay. Almost as much as you do. But here's the thing. Until you do, I have to take care of you."

Take care of me. Danny Malone was going to take care of me?

Hearing him say that—hearing anyone say that, let alone the boy I had yearned for when I was still a girl—oh, it was a beautiful moment.

"Chan? Would you mind getting off the cake plate?"

"Is that what I'm on?"

"Yeah. And there's some cake left, so . . ."

I suddenly realized I was hungry. And out of nowhere—well, out of my mouth, but without any conscious action—I saw a long white tongue shoot out and grab a crumb of chocolate cake.

"Yecch!" Danny shoved himself away from the table so violently he knocked his chair over.

"Oh, my God." I swallowed the crumb without chewing. "Did I do that? Was that my tongue?"

He righted his chair but didn't sit down. He stood next to the refrigerator like he didn't want to be anywhere near my tongue.

"Sorry," I said. "I guess that's how I eat." How humiliating. If I were human, I would have blushed.

"I guess I must look pretty disgusting," I said. And *snap!* There went my tongue again, for another cake crumb.

"Uh, no," he said carefully. "You're really pretty nice-looking. For a frog. Do you want to see yourself? There's a mirror in—"

"No! And I don't want anyone else to see me either." I hopped off the cake plate before my tongue could embarrass me again. "Hey, I just thought of something. When your parents get home—what happens then?"

"It's just my dad," Danny said. "And he's on assignment in Chicago. I'm not sure when he'll be back."

"There's no one else here?"

He shook his head. "Only Bobo."

Alone at last. Me and Danny Malone.

Somehow, it wasn't the way I'd always pictured it.

"You're an amphibian." Danny was reading from the *Junior Science Encyclopedia* he'd found on the bottom of his bookshelves. "Of the order Salientia, family Ranidae, genus *Rana*, species—"

"Do we really need all these gruesome details?" I cut in.

"I have to know what to feed you," he said, "and how much water you'll want. Different frogs have different requirements."

"Just fill the bathtub and phone for a pizza," I said. "Unless there's something in there about how to change frogs into humans, I'm not interested."

Danny shrugged. "Suit yourself." He kept on reading, but silently.

I started to explore his room. He was pretty sloppy. His bed was unmade. His closet door was open, revealing a jumble of hockey sticks, baseball mitts, hiking boots, and magazines.

A TV-VCR combination rested on a stand under the window. Videocassettes, CDs, and audiotapes spilled out of the storage compartment.

"You really *don't* ever clean up," I remarked.

"I wasn't expecting company," he said. "Come here for a minute."

I hopped onto the desk. "Did you find something?" I asked hopefully.

"I can't figure out if you're *Rana clamitans* or *Rana catesbeiana*," he said peering down at me.

"Speak English! And stop staring. You're making me self-conscious."

"You're larger than a green frog and smaller than a

bullfrog," he said.

"Who cares?"

"Well," he began, "if you're a bullfrog you eat mice, fish, lizards and—"

"Lizards? Mice? Are you out of your mind?"

"You don't have to chew them," he said. "You swallow them whole."

I leaped off the desk onto the top of the TV. "This discussion is over. I may look like a frog, but inside I'm still human. And I think I'm going to throw up."

"Not very likely," he disagreed. "Because your digestive system is—"

"If I had hands," I said, as loudly as I could, "I'd hold them over my ears. If I knew where my ears were."

"They're right behind your eyes," Danny said. "But they're on the inside. No openings. Isn't that weird?"

"Gee, I don't know, Danny," I said. "Considering everything else, finding out that my ears are on the inside doesn't strike me as particularly earth-shattering."

He turned to face me. "That was sarcasm again, right?"

"Right. Is *Oprah* on yet?"

"You're going to watch TV?" he asked.

"What do you expect me to do, knit?"

He slid his chair over to the TV and turned the set on. I jumped onto his bed.

"Can you see from there?" he asked. "Maybe you want to get closer? Or sit on a book or something?"

"I can see fine." Then I realized he was not worried about how well I could see. What bothered him was a frog lounging on his pillow.

I swallowed down more invisible tears and jumped onto the nightstand. "I can see okay from here too."

He flicked the remote a few times. "I don't know what's on now," he said. "I'm not usually home."

"It doesn't matter. This'll do." It was a talk show with a host I didn't recognize. A whole bunch of women were yelling insults at each other. The audience was hooting and whistling.

"We'll be right back!" The slick-haired host shoved his face at the camera. "With daughters who think their mothers are dowdy dressers!"

"Oh, good grief," I muttered.

I watched a string of commercials for lawyers, deodorant, Great Romantic Accordion Hits, and the Follicle Finder Hair-Removal System.

There's the upside of being a frog, I thought glumly. At least I don't have to worry about shaving my legs.

Bobo whuffled and whined in the hallway. He began scratching at the door.

"I'd better let him in," Danny said. "You'll have to get used to each other sooner or later."

I jumped on top of the TV. "I'd rather get used to him when I'm bigger than he is," I said.

Bobo leaped at Danny as soon as the door opened,

nearly knocking him over. I watched cautiously from my perch on the TV as Danny wrestled him to the floor. They rolled around the room in a pretend battle.

"I hope he won't want to do that with me," I said.

At the sound of my croak, Bobo's ears pricked up. He shook his head to clear the hair out of his eyes, and looked around for the source of the voice.

"I don't think this apartment is big enough for the both of us," I said.

"You'll be fine," Danny said. "As soon as you're in your aquarium."

"Aquarium?" I repeated. "You're going to put me in a cage?"

"Not a cage," Danny said. "It's glass, like a fish tank. I'll put in some moss, and rocks for you to sit on, and water—it'll be like a vacation in the Bahamas."

"I've been to the Bahamas!" I said. "They don't have glass around them!"

"As long as you're a frog," he said, "you're going to have to live like a frog. I don't want you to die."

"I do," I said miserably.

"No you don't. I'm going to run a tub so you can swim for a while. You've been out of water too long already."

"Hey! I just remembered something," I said. "I can't swim."

Danny lifted me off the TV. "I'll bet you can now."

FOUR

"I wonder what temperature the water should be." Danny placed me on the edge of the tub. "Cold, I guess, since you're cold-blooded."

"I'm not cold-blooded," I disagreed. "I'm just reserved."

He ran a couple of inches of water into the tub.

"I like bubbles," I said. "And bath oil."

"No bubbles. No oil. You don't want to gunk up your skin. You get oxygen through it."

"How charming," I said. "I'm a skin-breather. Hey, this isn't a Jacuzzi, is it?" In my condition, a Jacuzzi would be the equivalent of a giant blender.

He turned off the faucet. "It's not a Jacuzzi. Go on, hop in."

"I'm telling you, I can't swim," I insisted. "I'll drown."

"You won't drown," he said. "You can jump at least ten feet. If you think you're in trouble, just hop onto the faucet."

"Survival camp would have been a snap compared to this," I muttered.

"What?"

"Never mind." I took a deep breath. "I wish I could hold my nose," I said. "If I have a nose."

"You have two little nostrils, right—"

"Oh, shut up!" I leaped into the tub. I landed with a little splash, and immediately felt my back legs stretch out. "Whoo!" I started gliding through the water, my legs propelling me along in a smooth, even path.

"Hey, I'm doing it! I'm doing it!" I started to go faster, reached the end of the tub, swooped around, and sped back the other way. "Whee! This is neat!"

I was able to keep the top of my head above the water, so I didn't even get my eyes or nose wet. (If I had a nose.) Danny leaned over to watch as I zoomed around the tub.

What a spectacle I must be making of myself, I realized. What was I thinking of, letting him see me like this?

With as much dignity as I could muster—considering the position I was in—I paddled behind the shower curtain. "Excuse me," I said, "but could I have a little privacy here? I'm taking a bath."

After Danny left, I did a few more laps around the tub. But the thrill of discovering my new ability was wearing off. I began to wonder what I looked like. What did Danny see when he looked at me?

I didn't really want to know. I'm a frog, I told myself. How good can I look?

Maybe I'd be better off not knowing, I thought. I sat shivering in the tub, afraid to see what I had turned into.

Finally my curiosity overcame my fear. I jumped onto the rim of the tub. There was a full-length mirror on the back of the bathroom door. I took a deep breath, and looked.

"Aagghh!"

"What is it? Danny shouted. He threw the bathroom door open. "What's the matter?"

"I'm a frog!" I wailed.

"You knew that already," he said.

"But I didn't realize—I mean, till I looked in the mirror I still felt like myself."

"You are yourself," he said." Except you're green. And you can swim." He opened the bathtub drain.

"Don't let the water out," I said. "I want to drown myself."

"No you don't." When the water was gone he took me into the kitchen. I watched as he snapped Bobo's leash on. "He needs a walk," Danny said. "And I'll get some supplies for your aquarium while I'm out."

"Goody," I said. "Hey! Get a pizza too. Suddenly I'm really hungry."

"You don't eat pizza," he said. "You're a carnivore. You eat bugs and fish."

"So get an anchovy pizza."

With Danny and Bobo gone, I had a chance to look around. It was a relief to be by myself for a while, to get more adjusted to my body without someone watching me.

I found that I didn't have to jump to get places. I could walk—sort of—moving my opposite arm and leg. But it was slow going, and I imagined I must look like a reptile slithering around like that. Jumping, I concluded, was the way to go.

I wondered what I might be able to do with my skinny little fingers. Maybe I could manipulate things like the TV remote, or even a computer. Maybe I could put food in my mouth with my fingers, instead of grabbing it with my tongue. Mealtimes would certainly be more pleasant that way. At least for Danny.

And if I could manage to turn pages, I might be able to read!

I jumped onto the coffee table in front of the sofa. I landed on a copy of *The Midnight Rambler,* one of those sleazy supermarket tabloids. Danny reads this junk? I thought.

I could make out the headlines pretty easily. "MAN GROWS 42-INCH TOENAIL!" "LOSE 20 POUNDS ON MIRACLE PORK RIND DIET!!" "ELVIS'S SECRET PRAYER MEETINGS WITH THE DALAI LAMA!!!"

I tried to turn the page. But I couldn't, because my fingers (I would *not* call them claws) wouldn't grasp the thin paper. But I could push with them, so I dragged at the front page and shoved the paper open with my head.

Staring out at me were two pictures, one of a very fat

woman and one of a very thin woman. Over them the headline read: "SHE LOST 80 POUNDS EATING PORK RINDS AND SO CAN YOU!" By Joe Malone.

"Melody Layne Petherbridge of Indio, Texas," the article began, "is half the woman she was a year ago, thanks to a diet that features her favorite snack food, fried pork—"

Joe *Malone*? J. Malone! Danny's father?

"Oh, no!" What if he finds out about me? What if he wants to do an article about me? How could he *not* want to do an article about me?

It was too hideous to think about—and too easy to imagine.

"FROG GIRL BAFFLES SCIENCE!! SHE WALKS, SHE TALKS, SHE SLITHERS ON HER BELLY LIKE A REPTILE!" By Joe Malone.

"Chandler Brooks of Pelham, New York, is 1/16th the girl she was yesterday, all because she let a classmate . . ."

I think I screamed.

If *The Midnight Rambler* thought a forty-two-inch toenail was hot stuff, wait till they heard about me.

FIVE

"How does it taste?" Danny asked.

We were sitting in the kitchen, me on top of the refrigerator, Bobo next to Danny's chair. We were all eating pizza. Danny had cut mine into little pieces. I was able to pick them up with my fingers, but my tongue still flicked out to grab the food. Which was why I decided to eat on top of the refrigerator.

"I have no idea," I said. "I don't think I chew, just swallow. The anchovies are nice and salty though."

"I hate anchovies," he said.

"How tragic," I said. "What a rough life you have."

"I was just making conversation," he said.

"Don't make conversation," I said. "Make plans. Like how to turn me back into a person before your father finds out about me."

"I stopped at the library," Danny said. "I got a copy of *The Frog Prince*."

"What for?"

"I thought it might give us an idea about what turned you into a frog."

"We know what turned me into a frog," I said. "You kissed me."

"I've kissed other girls," he said, "and none of them turned into frogs. Plus, the story might give us an idea of what happens to change the frog back into a prince."

"But that's a fairy tale," I said. "This is real life."

Danny held out his hands. "We have to start somewhere."

He dumped our paper plates into the garbage and put the leftover pizza in the refrigerator. He pulled a large book from his backpack. On the cover was a picture of a frog wearing a gold crown.

"'Once upon a time . . .'"

I listened as he read the story aloud. Bobo went to sleep under the table.

"That's not what happened to me," I said when he finished reading. "The frog turned into a person when the princess kissed him. I started out as a person and turned into a frog."

"He was a person too," Danny said, "before the story began. He was a prince till an evil spell turned him into a frog."

"But I was never a frog, till this afternoon."

"I think the point here," Danny said, "is that the spell

was broken when someone finally saw behind his outer ugliness. The princess kissed him because she recognized that he was good inside."

"So if you go by the story," I said, "I have to find somebody who wants to kiss me because he likes me, not because someone bet him a dollar he couldn't."

"Yeah, well, uh . . ." Danny said lamely.

"What do you think my chances of that are?"

"I'll go get your aquarium ready."

Danny had found an old fish tank in the basement storage room. He washed it off and set it on his desk. "You'll get lots of sunshine here," he pointed out. "Frogs like to bask in the sun."

"Don't you know that getting sunburned is one of the most dangerous things you can do?" Was it only a few hours ago that I'd heard Lauren say that?

"Trust me," Danny said. "You won't get a sunburn. You have real tough skin."

"I need it," I said, without thinking.

"What do you mean?"

"Never mind. Forget it." Bobo paced back and forth in front of the TV, never taking his eyes off me.

"Is my cage ready yet?" I asked. "I think your dog is still hungry."

"All done." Danny put a large, flat rock into the tank.

"And it's not a cage. I couldn't get any moss, but I found some potting soil."

"Oh, goody," I said. "Potting soil. What a nice change from wall-to-wall carpeting."

Danny picked me up and put me in the aquarium. "What do you think?"

I looked around. Dirt, rocks, a bowl of water large enough for me to sit in, glass walls boxing me in on all sides.

"Throw up some wallpaper, hang a few pictures, it'll be real cozy."

"Sarcasm again, right?" he asked. "Look, I'm doing the best I can."

"I wasn't being sarcastic," I said. "It was either make a joke or burst out crying."

"Ah, Chandler." He sank onto the desk chair and rubbed his eyes. "I'm trying to stay cheerful, and not get you any more upset than you already are, but . . ." His voice trailed off. He looked at me sadly. "I feel so helpless."

He reached into the tank and patted me gently on the head. In a minute I *would* burst into tears. Danny looked pretty close to the edge himself.

"That feels nice," I said. "I'd enjoy it even more if I was human."

The phone on his desk rang. I nearly jumped out of my (tough, green) skin.

Danny picked up the receiver.

"Hey, Dad, how're you doing? Oh, nothing much. How's it going in Chicago? He did? Italy? When will you be back? No, that's okay. No, I don't need Aunt Sally to—pizza. Okay, tomorrow I'll make a salad. Stop fussing, I'll be fine. You too. Bye."

"Well, we have a few more days," he said, as he hung up the phone. "He has to go to Italy for a convention of oxygen eaters."

"What are oxygenators?" I asked.

"Oxygen *eaters*," he corrected me. "They're people who don't need food. They say they can get all the nourishment they need from the air."

"Good grief."

"The guy he was interviewing in Chicago was on his way to a big convention of oxygen eaters in Italy. So my dad's going along. He won't be back till Tuesday."

"Three and a half days," I calculated. "I hope that's enough time."

"It better be," Danny said. "Journalists would kill for a story like yours."

"Jounalists!" I sneered. "That's not journalism. I'd be embarrassed if my father worked for one of those rags."

"What does your father do?" Danny asked.

"He's dead," I said.

"I'm sorry. What about your mother?"

"They're both dead."

"That's rough," he said sympathetically. "Don't you have any family at all?"

"Just my cousin, Horace."

"Hey!" Danny looked panicky. "What are we going to tell him? You can't just disappear like this."

"He's in Switzerland," I said. "And even if he weren't, I don't think he'd lose any sleep over me."

"There's no one else?" Danny asked.

"Just Mrs. Gruen, the housekeeper. She's got the week off."

"Is she nice?" he asked. "Do you like her?"

"Not particularly. She's a good cook, though."

He didn't say anything for a moment. Then, "You must get pretty lonely."

"Don't worry about my personal life," I snapped. I wanted this conversation to end. "Just figure out how to get me back to it by Tuesday."

"I guess," he said slowly, "you don't like most people."

"That's not true!" I must have said it loudly enough to scare Bobo. He stuck his nose against the side of the aquarium and tried to see me through his hair.

I gave a little shriek and hopped to the other side, away from his nose. "I just don't know that many people."

Bobo dragged his nose along the glass, leaving a long, wet smudge. "Will you make him stop that! He's smearing up my whole wall. It's *disgusting.*"

Danny got a tissue and wiped off the glass. "If you—I

mean *when* you turn back, I'll introduce you to lots of people. It's not hard to make friends."

"Yeah, yeah, right. For you, maybe." I jumped into my water bowl. He'd started to say "*If* you turn back." I couldn't bear to think that I might never change into myself again.

"But if we don't work on that attitude—" he began.

"Don't worry about my attitude!" I said. "That's not our first priority."

"All right, all right." He sighed. "Look, I've got a whole lot of research on frogs to do. Will you be okay by yourself for a while?"

"Sure, go ahead, leave me," I said sourly. "And take your little dog, too."

He paused at the door. "If you start shedding your skin, call me. I want to see that."

"Shedding my skin?" I stuck my head out of the water. "Why would I do that?"

"I don't know," he said. "You just do."

"And then what? I walk around in my bones? If I have bones?"

"There's other skin underneath," he said.

"What happens to my old skin?"

"Sometimes you eat it," he answered.

"Oh, *gross!* Eating my own . . . Hey! Are there any anchovies left?"

He hustled Bobo out of the room. I stayed in the water

bowl. The water felt silky and soothing on my body. I watched the light fade through the window as the second worst day of my life drew to a close.

What would happen to me if I never did change back? If I had to stay a frog for the rest of my life? And how long would the rest of my life be? Would I spend it here, in this glass prison, with Danny taking care of me like another pet? Or would he decide he ought to release me into the wild, to live among my own kind?

If it was hard to make friends when I was human, how in the world would I learn to get along with other frogs? I didn't even speak the language.

What if, as time passed, I grew less and less human and more and more amphibian? What if I actually developed a liking for flies and worms, and my human memories began to disappear, and I forgot I'd ever been a girl named Chandler?

The room grew dimmer. I jumped out of the bowl onto the potting soil. It was soft and cushiony.

If I did forget I'd been human, how would I know I'd forgotten? I wouldn't remember my former life. I wouldn't know what I'd lost and I couldn't miss what I didn't remember. I'd just live from fly to fly, operating on frog instincts, not knowing or caring that there was a world beyond my pond that I'd never see again.

I was getting sleepy.

Maybe the best thing that could happen would be to

turn completely frog. No more emotions. No more shyness or loneliness. No more blushing. I'd never feel self-conscious again. I'd never have to try and think of something clever to say. I wouldn't have to say anything. Except "ribbit."

All in all, I thought, as I drifted off to sleep, it might be easy being green.

SIX

The next thing I knew, sunlight was streaming through the window, and Danny was peering down into my aquarium.

"Aw, rats," I said. "I guess it wasn't a dream."

"Funny," said Danny. "That was the first thing I thought of this morning."

"It's tomorrow? I mean, it isn't today anymore? I mean—"

"I know what you mean," he cut in. "Waking up in a strange place can be confusing."

"I'm not a bit confused," I said. "Everything is all too clear."

"Are you hungry?"

"For what?" I asked suspiciously.

"Froot Loops?" he suggested. "Pop Tarts? Microwave chili?"

"Chili?" I stared at him coldly. "For breakfast?" But suddenly the thought of ground beef was appealing. In fact, chili was just what I wanted. In fact, I wanted it *immediately.*

"Sounds good," I said. "Be sure not to overheat it. And would you pick out the beans first?"

Danny had promised to help his aunt clean out her attic that morning.

"You're going to leave me alone with that dog?"

"I'll close the door so he can't get in," he said. "It'll only be for a few hours."

"A few *hours?* What am I supposed to do while you're gone?"

"Try hibernating," he said. "That's what most frogs do in the winter."

"I can't believe a messy attic is more important than I am."

"Chandler, if I don't go she'll come here to check up on me. You'll be fine. I'll be back before you know it."

With Danny gone the apartment felt empty and lifeless. The hours till he'd return stretched before me like blank pages waiting to be filled.

How was I going to fill them? What did frogs do all day? My water bowl was too small for swimming. Even if there were any flies in the room, I had no interest in catching them with my tongue. I wasn't sleepy enough to hibernate.

I jumped out of the aquarium onto the desk chair. Maybe if I got a little exercise I'd tire myself out enough to fall asleep. Hop till you drop, I told myself.

I still wasn't too good at judging distances though. Aiming for the windowsill, I landed on the TV, knocking a bunch of tapes off the top.

"Oops."

I jumped for the bookcase, curious to see what kind of books Danny read. I crashed into a framed photograph on the top shelf. It flew across the room and smashed against a dresser.

"Oops."

Bobo started barking.

Well, so much for hopping till I dropped. With the broken glass on the floor, and my limited spatial assessment skills, I was afraid to risk any more exercise.

But I didn't want to stay on the bookcase all morning. I was sure I could reach the bed, since I'd done it the day before, so I took one last, mighty leap.

I overshot the bed and banged into the clock radio on the nightstand. It skidded into a lamp. The lamp fell over and tumbled off the stand.

"Oops."

Suddenly loud rock music blasted my ears. I'd accidentally turned the radio on. Bobo went berserk.

Between his hysterical barking and the blare of the music I thought my head would explode. "Be quiet!" I shouted.

I found the "on/off" button and pressed it with my little green hand. The music stopped. Bobo quieted down, but I could still hear him panting and snuffling at the door.

I carefully jumped onto the bed. I landed on something that didn't feel like bed—something hard with little bumps. The next thing I knew, the TV was on at full volume, and Bobo was howling again.

For Pete's sake, the whole room was booby-trapped. Gingerly I pushed myself off the bumpy thing, which turned out to be the TV remote.

"All right!" I said. "I bet I can handle this." Bobo yelped and banged against the door. *"Will you shut up, you miserable hairball!"*

I found I could press the mute button with my fingers but it was hard to adjust the sound level. Pushing channels up and down was easy, and soon I learned how much pressure to use on the volume control.

Bobo eventually settled down and I started channel-surfing.

The *Donna Draper* show was on channel 2. Six women were sitting in a row of chairs, screaming at six guys. The graphic on the screen read "*He leaves his clothes all over the floor!*"

I pushed the "channel up" button.

"Today, on the *Charlie Sawyer* show! Siamese twins in love with the same woman!"

Click. Channel 5. The *Misty Blake* show. Misty Blake was standing next to a shirtless guy in a black leather vest.

His arms, chest, and neck were crawling with tattoos of writhing snakes.

Misty turned to the girl at his side. "So, Rhonda," she said, "what is it about Elroy's tatoos that turns you off?"

There must be *something* else on, I told myself.

There wasn't.

I settled for "Haircut Horror Stories," though in my condition the topic wasn't exactly relevant. "Haircut Horror Stories" was followed by "People Who Like to Set Fire to Things," which was followed by "Diet Disasters."

At that point my eyes glazed over. Mercifully, I dozed off.

"What happened in here?"

I woke abruptly.

Danny stood in the doorway of his room surveying the destruction.

"I'm sorry," I said. "See, what happened was, I got bored, and—"

"So you decided to trash my room?"

"I didn't *decide* the trash your room," I said indignantly. "It was an accident. Okay, a couple of accidents. Besides, your room wasn't that neat to begin with."

"For crying out loud, Chandler." He bent down and started picking up pieces of broken glass.

"Be careful," I warned. "Don't cut yourself."

"Thanks for the safety tip," he muttered.

"You know, I was just going to tell you how glad I was to see you," I began. "But if you're going to take that attitude . . ." I *was* glad to see him, no matter what his attitude was. There was life in the apartment now, and someone to talk to. And someone to take care of me.

He got a broom and dustpan and swept up the glass. He set the lamp back on the nightstand. "I'll have to get a new bulb," he grumbled.

"What a tedious job that will be," I said. "I hope it doesn't spoil your whole vacation."

"You've already taken care of that," he snapped.

"This is not exactly how I planned to spend midwinter break either," I said. Suddenly I realized I was hungry. Really, really hungry. "What's for lunch? And can we have it now?"

He snatched me off his bed and plopped me into the aquarium. "You've got plenty of chili left."

"What's the matter with you? Why are you being so nasty?"

He picked up the photograph, now with a bent frame and no glass, and put it on his bookcase. "This was my mother's picture."

"I said I'm sorry," I repeated. "I'll buy you a new frame. I'll buy you a new lightbulb."

"You can't solve everything with money, Chandler."

"Tell me about it!" I almost laughed.

He stacked the videotapes back on the TV stand. "I

can't take much more of this," he said. "You're destroying the house, you're making my dog crazy, and you're blaming me because you turned into a frog."

"How you suffer," I tsked. "And here I've been having such a dandy time."

"That's another thing I'm getting tired of," he said. "For a shy person you sure have a big mouth."

"I didn't have a big mouth when I was a person," I said. "And I'm a lot more scared of your dog than he is of me. And, for the last time, I didn't mess up your room on purpose."

"I didn't change you into a frog on purpose!" he said. "But you're still blaming me."

"Because it's your fault," I said. "And you're the only one who can help me change back. I don't suppose you got any brilliant ideas while you were cleaning your aunt's attic?"

"I got an idea," he said slowly. "I don't know how brilliant it is. And I'm sure you're not going to like it."

"If it'll change me back into a person I'll love it. What's the idea?"

"It came to me when we were eating lunch," he said. "We were watching one of those talk shows—"

"No!" I cried. "Not that!"

"There was this pair of Siamese twins—"

"NO! *Never!*"

He went right on as if he hadn't heard me. ". . . and

my aunt said, 'Can you believe how many people watch these programs?' And I said, 'I guess all the people that read my father's paper.' Which is a lot of people."

I leaped into my water bowl, as if I could hide there.

"What else can we do?" he asked. "We have to go public. Somewhere out there someone might be watching who can help us."

"I'd sooner die!"

"No you wouldn't."

"I might as well," I said. "I'll be a freak. I'll be a spectacle. I'll be Page One in *The Midnight Rambler. Hot Flash* will do a dramatic re-creation of me!"

Hot Flash was the grossest show on TV. It was as bad as *The Midnight Rambler.* They featured people abducted by space aliens, alleged mob hitmen, and women who claimed to be the abandoned daughters of political candidates.

I jumped out of the water bowl and started hopping back and forth across the aquarium. "And if I ever do turn back into a person," I went on, "I'll never have a moment's peace."

"But Chandler, if you want to—"

"I'll always be Frog Girl! Kids'll hound me to say "ribbit" for them. They'll put bugs in my lunch. Twenty years from now someone will write a book called *Whatever Happened to Frog Girl?* I'll never live it down!"

"What choice do we have?" Danny said. "The only other

thing I can think of is to ask every guy I know to kiss you and see if one of them can change you back."

"That might work," I said hopefully.

"But a lot of people are away this week," he reminded me. "And even the ones that are home . . ." He held his hands out. "How many do you think I could get to kiss a frog?"

"Mason Gorman got you to kiss me for a dollar," I said.

"You were a girl," he said. "I wouldn't have kissed a frog for a dollar."

I sighed. "Neither would I."

"Look, if we can get on a talk show, nobody will know who you are."

I thought about that for a moment. "You're probably right. I don't look at all like myself."

"Not at all," he agreed.

"And they say the camera adds ten pounds," I went on.

"And you could use a fake name," he said. He reached into his back pocket and pulled out a folded magazine. "I bought this on the way home. It has phone numbers for all the talk shows." He unfolded it so I could see the cover.

"It tells the kinds of guests they're looking for," he said. "I checked off a bunch we can try."

"You have been a busy little beaver, haven't you?"

"Well, how about it?" he asked. "Should I start calling?"

"I have a feeling," I said, "even if nobody recognizes

me, this will probably be the most embarrassing experience of my life."

"Would you rather be a frog?" he asked.

"Start phoning."

SEVEN

"Aw, no, not *Hot Flash,*" I begged. "Tell me you didn't get us on *Hot Flash.*"

"They were the only ones who were interested," Danny said.

"But it's such an awful program."

"The important thing is to get you out there and see if there's someone who can help us," he reminded me. "And no one's going to know it's you. Did you think up a name yet?"

"Natasha," I said. "I've always loved that name."

"Natasha?" he repeated. "What kind of a name is that for a frog?"

"A romantic, mysterious name," I retorted.

"Okay, okay. Be Natasha."

Something small and white fluttered over my water bowl. "Is that a moth?" I asked. Before he could answer

I snagged it with my tongue and popped it into my mouth.

"Chandler! Ucchh!"

"What do you want from me?" I complained. "I'm a frog. And I'm getting tired of chili."

"I know," he said. "I'm sorry. But, listen . . . try not to do that on TV."

Monday afternoon we took the bus to Manhattan. Danny carried me in his backpack. There was a mesh pocket I fit into, so I could breathe. The weather had turned wintry again, so he'd wrapped me in a thick cotton sock to keep me warm.

It was a ten-block walk from the bus terminal to the TV studio. The noise and the crowds and the traffic fumes were overwhelming. Even with my pocket securely closed, I felt small and helpless. I was so little, and in such a huge place.

Danger lurked at every crosswalk. Cabs and buses and dog walkers and cyclists and impatient pedestrians were enemies who could crush me in an instant.

I had no nervous energy to spare for stage fright. It was all I could do to keep from swelling up so much that I'd burst through the pocket.

We entered a large, gray glass building. Danny gave his name to someone, who pointed to an elevator. He pulled his backpack off and turned it around so we could see each other.

"Here we go," he whispered.

On the forty-fourth floor we were directed to a large office with a horseshoe-shaped desk in the center. A bunch of other people sat on couches and chairs in the reception area. I couldn't see them too well from where I was.

We sat down opposite a woman holding a Siamese cat.

The woman at the desk called out, "Kid with the frog. Snap will see you now."

Snap Chapman, the host of *Hot Flash,* was sitting in a big leather chair when we were ushered into his office. He was eating something out of a white cardboard container. There were three other containers on his desk. I smelled shrimp.

"Where's the frog?" he asked.

Danny took me out of the backpack and placed me on the desk next to the food cartons.

Snap Chapman stared down at me, his beady little eyes glittering, his extravagant mustache twitching.

"What does it say?" he asked.

"What do you want me to say?" I said.

He dropped the container. He jumped up, knocking his chair into the wall behind him. "Holy—"

He moved cautiously back to the desk and bent over me. "Say something else," he ordered.

"The rain in Spain stays mainly on the plain."

He looked up at Danny. "That's pretty good. I didn't even see your lips move."

"I'm not doing it," Danny said. "I told you. The frog talks."

"Yeah, sure," Mr. Chapman said. "Listen, kid, I've seen it all. And most of it's a crock."

"I am not a crock," I declared.

He laughed and smacked his knee. "Great, great," he said. "Try and use that on the show."

"You mean, you'll put us on?" Danny asked.

"I don't know who's putting who on," Snap said. "But we'll try a taping and see what happens. Can he do anything else?"

"What more do you want me to do?" I demanded. "Isn't a talking frog amazing enough? And by the way, I'm a *she*. Natasha."

Snap gave Danny a just between-the-two-of-us smile. "Look, we both know there's some kind of trick to this. You think you're the first person to try and sell me a talking animal? I've got a Siamese cat coming in who's supposed to be a regular Chatty Cathy."

"If you think it's just a trick," Danny said, "why do you want us on the show?"

"We're in the entertainment business," Snap answered. "Of course," he added quickly, "we also have a commitment to inform and educate our viewers. But hey—ratings are the name of the game. We didn't get to be number one in our time slot by covering drought and famine."

"Speaking of famine," I said, eying the containers of food that surrounded me, "are you going to eat all this?"

One of Snap's assistants took us into Makeup.

"I don't want to wear makeup," Danny objected.

"That's up to you," the assistant said. "But you'll photograph a lot better with it. The lights are very harsh."

"I don't care how I look," he said.

"I do," I said. "I always wanted longer eyelashes."

The makeup woman nearly jumped out of her smock.

I hopped onto the counter and stared at myself in the lighted mirror. How depressing. I looked just like a frog. "Maybe a little color in my cheeks?" I suggested. "I look so *green.*"

The makeup woman tossed her brushes on the counter and ran out of the room.

Snap's assistant grinned at Danny. "You'll be great."

She led us out to the set. Snap told Danny to put me down on a low table between a pair of brown armchairs. There was a pitcher of water and two glasses on the table. Snap sat in one of the chairs, riffling through a sheaf of notes. He motioned Danny to the other chair.

"Now, don't be nervous," he said. "Just tell your story the way you told it to my producer when you called. But let the frog do most of the talking. That's what we're paying for."

"You're getting paid for this?" I said.

Snap glanced from me to Danny.

"Just the standard fee," Danny said.

"I thought you were doing this to help me!"

Snap gave a nervous little giggle. "Hey, kids—I mean, kid. Save it for the show."

"You're using me!" I fumed. "I should have known. You kissed me to win a measly dollar. Imagine how much you're going to make on me now!"

"Hey, hey." Snap's notes dropped to the floor as he stood. "What're you trying to pull here? Are you holding out for more money?"

"No, no," Danny said. "She's just a little—uh—sensitive. About her appearance. I mean, even before she turned into a frog she—"

"Ready to roll, Snap!" a voice called from somewhere behind the lights.

I was furious. I felt tricked, betrayed, exploited. I'd been so grateful that Danny was worrying about me, taking care of me, trying his best to help me get back to my own body. And all along he'd just been scheming to cash in on me.

"Why is she puffing up like that?" Snap asked uneasily.

"Frogs do that when they're upset," Danny said. He leaned over so he could whisper. "Chan, don't blow it."

I flicked my tongue at him. He jerked his head back.

"Rolling tape!" someone yelled.

Snap Chapman scooped his notes off the floor. He eyed me nervously. I didn't even try to un-swell myself. I was too angry.

"Tonight," he began, his voice cracking a little, "exclusive to *Hot Flash!* What may be the most amazing human transformation story in the history of the world!"

Just how much were they paying Danny to be on this trashy program? Did he need the money that badly?

". . . a classic fairy tale come to life?" Snap was saying. "Or simply an extraordinary achievement in animal-human communication? You be the judge."

Danny told the story of how he'd kissed me and changed me into a frog. I barely listened. I just sat there, my temper growing hotter than the blazing lights.

He's not going to get away with it, I thought. He's not going to use me this way.

I felt like people had been using me ever since my parents died. Cousin Horace wanted custody of me so he could use my inheritance. The housekeepers he hired kept me fed and clothed because they got paid to, not because they cared about what I ate or wore. Even Lauren and Kelly, my only friends, probably liked my pool more than they liked me.

And now Danny, the boy who had kissed me for a dollar, was looking for the big bucks.

This was the last straw.

". . . a truly astonishing story," Snap Chapman was

saying. "And I understand that you're appearing exclusively on *Hot Flash* in the hopes that someone, somewhere, will be able to turn Natasha back into the lovely young girl she was just a few short days ago."

"That's right," Danny said. "If it's okay, could I give my phone number? So anyone who thinks they can help will be able to call?"

"Certainly," Snap said. "We here at *Hot Flash* will do anything we can to help return this poor frog's life to normal."

Danny announced his phone number. Snap repeated it twice. "Now," he said, "let's hear what Natasha has to say."

He leaned over and smiled his smarmy smile at me. "Natasha, tell me, what will you do if you can never become a human being again?"

This was not something I wanted to think about—not with this oily media hack leering at me, not knowing what I now knew about the boy my life depended on. But that isn't why I didn't answer him.

"Natasha," Snap urged, "we want to hear your side of the story. Straight from the frog's mouth, so to speak."

"Chan—I mean, Natasha!" Danny grabbed me and held me close to his lips. "You've got to say something," he whispered. "This is our only hope."

How desperate he sounded. What a performance, I thought.

I stared at him coldly.

"Ribbit," I croaked, and jumped into the water pitcher.

EIGHT

Danny ranted at me all the way to the bus terminal. I couldn't hear a lot of what he was saying, because of the din of the city around us, and because I was strapped to his back facing behind him.

I could tell from the expressions of the people who passed us that they thought he was talking to himself. But a guy muttering wildly to nobody on 42nd Street was not such an unusual occurrence. Passersby just gave him as wide a berth as possible on the crowded sidewalk.

He was silent on the bus ride home, and so was I. In fact, I was taking a vow of silence. I would never speak to Danny again.

I started to plan what I would do if I ever turned back into myself. I wanted to ditch every person in my life who didn't really care about me.

First, I'd hire a lawyer and find a way to get Horace

un-declared my guardian. I'd fire Mrs. Gruen. Then I'd cement over the swimming pool and see if Kelly and Lauren still wanted to be my friends.

I could end up with nobody, I realized. But would I be any more alone than I already was?

When we got back to the apartment, Bobo hurled himself at Danny, barking joyfully. Danny shrugged off the backpack and dropped it on the bed in his room. He didn't say a word as he opened my pocket and carried me over to the aquarium.

That was fine with me. There was nothing he could say that I wanted to hear.

Although . . . Now that I'd resolved to sweep all the false friends and relatives out of my life, the flames of my anger were beginning to die down. Leaving me with a feeling of . . . intense hunger.

But I had my pride. No matter how hungry I got, I wasn't going to ask Danny to feed me. I wouldn't give him the satisfaction.

Maybe he'd remember how often I needed to eat and at least have the decency to nuke a pot pie for me.

An electric can opener whirred in the kitchen. Bobo's nails tapped on the tile floor. I heard his dish sliding around, and slurping sounds as he wolfed his food.

I wondered how dog food tasted. I wondered if Bobo would leave any over.

"Come on, fella," Danny said, after the sliding and slurping sounds stopped. "Time for your walk."

I heard footsteps and pawsteps, and the apartment door slammed.

You heartless, irresponsible, two-faced human! I thought bitterly. I ought to go out and live among my own kind, in the wilds of nature. At least out there there'd be plenty of worms and grubs and beetles . . . maybe even some nice, fat slugs.

Eeuwww. How could I think of eating slugs? I was even more rattled a moment later when I realized that the thought of snacking on a slug did not disgust me.

I've got to get out of here. I hopped fretfully around my aquarium. I'm losing touch with my inner human.

I jumped onto the desk. Luckily Danny hadn't closed his door. I hopped out of his room into the kitchen. I looked around for Bobo's dinner dish.

There was nothing on the floor but his water bowl.

I jumped onto the table. I saw a bowl of fruit at one end, with a few apples and some sad-looking grapes. I hopped up to the rim of the bowl, perched on an apple, and started flicking grapes into my mouth. Six of them filled me up.

Now what do I do? I wondered.

I'd already made plans for my human life—though I didn't have a clue as to how or when I'd get back to it. And I didn't want to do frog stuff. I needed to hold on to as much of my person-ness as I could.

Reading? Turning pages was hit or miss, even if I could manage to pull a book from the shelves. Writing my autobiography was out of the question until I could hold a pen. I could probably manage a phone, but who would I call?

TV seemed to be the only thing left.

I hopped into the living room. There was a big-screen TV in one corner. I jumped out onto the coffee table and saw the remote control. I pressed the power button. I hopped onto the couch, nudged over a throw pillow, and perched on it.

Snap Chapman's face filled the screen.

"Tonight! Exclusive to *Hot Flash!* The midget who claims that the N.Y.P.D.'s height requirement is keeping him off the force. Plus, an exclusive *Hot Flash* preview of the shocking new movie *Vampires for Breakfast.* And an exclusive interview with its sensational star, Brad Stone!

"But first: They talk to the animals, and the animals talk back!"

How could the show be on now? I wondered. We'd been there two hours ago. Then I remembered that the program was on tape.

The woman I'd seen in the waiting room with the Siamese cat was sitting on one of the brown chairs next to Snap Chapman.

"*Hot Flash* welcomes Alexandra Dupree, and her cat, Mee Tu," Snap announced. "You know, Alexandra, a lot of people come to us claiming their animals can talk. Tragically, all of these individuals have been fakes and con persons."

I hissed at the screen. I knew when I'd been insulted.

Ms. Dupree shook her head disapprovingly. "I don't understand how people think they can get away with things like that," she said. "Especially with a hard-nosed investigative reporter like yourself."

Snap Chapman tried to smile modestly. He failed.

After some buildup, and a string of commercials, Snap said, "Okay, Alexandra, let's hear from Mee Tu."

Ms. Dupree held the cat up under its front paws, facing the camera. "Mee Tu," she said, "do you want to talk to Snap now or later?"

"Nyoww," the cat said.

"Oh, come on!" I shouted. But the camera moved in for a closeup of Snap's face. He was, apparently, astonished.

"That's incredible!" he exclaimed.

"Mee Tu," Ms. Dupree went on, "who do you think was the most important world leader of the twentieth century?"

"Maaoo," the cat answered.

Snap Chapman appeared stunned. "Does he mean Mao Tse-tung?" Snap asked. "Is Mee Tu a *communist?*"

"Oh, no!" Ms. Dupree answered quickly. "He's completely nonpolitical. It's just that he was born in China, so naturally—"

"Fake!" I screamed. "Phony! Liar!"

To think, that scam artist had bounced us off his show and put on this lame excuse for a talking animal instead.

But whose fault was that? I asked myself. When the time had come to put my mouth where the money was, I'd refused to *be* a talking animal.

"Mee Tu," Ms. Dupree went on, "if someone steps on your tail, who gets hurt, and what does he say?"

"Me—OW!"

"Fraud!" I yelled. "You're not talking, you're meowing!"

I never even heard the apartment door open. But the sounds of shrill yapping and the galumphing of four hairy paws alerted me.

Bobo hurled himself at the couch. I leaped over him. He landed sprawled across the sofa, sending throw pillows flying in all directions. I ended up in a pot of ivy, on a wrought-iron plant stand.

"Get him away from me!"

"You're finally talking," Danny said grimly.

"I'm not talking!" I screamed. "I'm screaming. I always scream when my life is in danger."

"Why didn't you stay in your aquarium, where you belong?"

"I am not speaking to you," I said, from a tangle of ivy.

"I'm not very fond of you right now, either," Danny said.

"You were never fond of me!" I poked my head through the ivy and glared at him. "No one was ever fond of me! You're just the latest person in a long line of people who aren't fond of me!"

"What are you talking about?" he asked. "And why are

you talking about it now? Why didn't you talk when it could have done us some good?"

"Done *us* some good? Give me a break."

Bobo was now pacing back and forth next to the plant stand, his one visible eye fixed intently on me.

"Chandler, what is your *problem?*" Danny asked.

"Surely you jest."

"I mean, your attitude problem," he said. "Ever since I've known you—"

"You've only known me since you turned me into a frog," I interrupted. "*You* try being small and green and living in a fish tank, and worrying what you're going to eat, or what's going to eat you, and see what *your* attitude is."

"Okay, okay, I get the point," Danny admitted. "But I never wanted to go on *Hot Flash* for the money. I didn't even know they paid when I called them."

He took Bobo by the collar and led him out of the room. I heard a door close, then some whimpering and scratching.

"Come out of the flowerpot," Danny said, when he returned to the living room. "He's locked up."

"Thank you." I worked my way through the ivy leaves and hopped onto the windowsill.

"Do you want something to eat?" he asked.

"No, thank you."

"That's a first," Danny said.

"I took some grapes," I told him. "When you left me to forage for myself."

"How about a swim? Should I run a bath for you?"

"Don't go to any trouble on my account," I said coolly. "I had better learn self-reliance."

"Chandler, don't be that way. I understand how you feel, but—"

"No man understands how I feel," I said, "until he has walked a mile in my—uh—whatever."

"I was going to split the money with you."

"I don't need money!" I shouted. "I've got too much money already! What I need is to not be a frog!"

He sighed. "I don't know what else to do."

I spotted a ladybug on the windowsill. I scooped it up with my tongue and swallowed it.

"I'll go run the bath water," he said hastily.

Danny sat next to the tub with his back to me as I glided through the water. It was cool and soothing. I felt myself grow calmer.

"I'm enjoying this too much," I muttered.

"What do you mean?"

"I'm afraid I'm becoming more and more frog," I said.

"You are a frog." He shrugged. "Why deny yourself a few froggy pleasures?"

"I'm only a frog on the outside," I said. "Inside I'm a girl. And I'm scared that I'll lose my human abilities."

"You can still talk," Danny pointed out. "Too bad I'm the only one who knows that."

"Yeah, well, I was angry," I said. "I couldn't help it. All my life—" I stopped myself.

"All your life what?" he asked.

"Nothing. Never mind."

He turned around so he could see me. "What? Tell me."

"Do you *mind?*" I snapped. "You promised not to look."

"Chandler, you haven't worn clothes since you've been a frog. What difference does it make if you're in the tub?"

"A person's modesty ought to be respected," I told him. "Even if that person is a frog."

"All right, I won't look." He turned his back on me again. "What did you mean when you said you had too much money?"

I couldn't answer him right away.

I'd been hiding for such a long time. I'd spent so many years pretending not to know, not to care. And it had only been three hours since I'd realized I couldn't fool myself anymore.

And Danny had already seen all of me. At least, my outside. What was left to cover up?

So I told him. How my parents were killed, what my life was like, with Horace and the series of housekeepers he'd hired to stay with me so that he wouldn't have to.

I even told him that he was the first person who'd kissed me in five years.

"And look how that turned out," I finished.

"I don't know what to say." He shook his head.

"You don't have to say anything." I hopped out of the water onto the edge of the tub. "It feels good to finally tell someone."

"What about Kelly and Lauren?" he asked. "They're your friends."

"I can't help thinking they might not be my friends if I didn't have such a neat pool."

"That's dumb, Chandler. You're not the only person in town with a pool. And they don't just hang out with you in the summer, do they?"

"It's heated," I said. "And enclosed."

"Hey, that does sound neat," he said.

"See?"

"How come you have a pool if you can't swim?" he asked.

"Horace can. You see what I mean?" I went on. "Then I find out that you're making money for getting me on *Hot Flash*. What am I supposed to think?"

Danny opened the drain and let the water out of the tub. "I miss my mother," he said abruptly.

"Did she die?"

"No, she just left. Walked out. When I was six."

"Why?"

He shrugged. "She said she wasn't cut out to be a wife and mother. She needed a different kind of life."

"That's awful!" At least my parents hadn't wanted to leave me.

He picked me up and carried me back to the aquarium. He sat down at the desk. "I just wanted you to know," he said, "that I do understand how you feel. Even if you think I don't."

"It's good that you still have your father," I said.

"Yeah, and he's great," Danny said. "But he travels so much. I'm alone a lot too. Like you."

The phone rang. I jumped, startled, and banged into the wall of the aquarium. "Ouch!"

"That must be him now," Danny said, reaching for the receiver. "Are you okay?"

"I'd feel better if I could rub my nose," I said. "If I have a nose."

"I'll rub it for you when I get off the phone," he said.

"I'll look forward to it." I climbed onto my rock.

"Hi, Dad, I knew it was—what?" He frowned. "How did you get my number? You do? Really? When? Sure, sure we can! That'll be great! Okay. See you tomorrow."

He hung up the phone. He punched his fist into the air. *"Yes!"*

"What?" I asked. *"What?"*

"You're not going to believe this," he said. "But we're back in show business."

NINE

Misty Blake was an actress who'd played troubled teenagers in a few lame TV movies. Now she had a live afternoon talk show. In fact, I had seen about ten seconds of it the other day, when she was interviewing the guy with the snake tatoos.

As Danny explained it, Misty's producer, Jill, was friendly with Snap Chapman's assistant. After Snap kicked us off the set, the assistant got Danny's phone number from the tape and called Jill.

On Tuesday, we'd had an interview with Misty and Jill, and they were so impressed they changed their scheduled lineup for Wednesday to put us on the show.

Now, here we were, in the greenroom—a very appropriate place for me, I thought—waiting for the program to start.

There was a long buffet table against one wall, loaded with goodies—cookies, nuts, fruit, cheese, vegetables, and dip. I hopped around it, looking for something I could eat.

"Snap's assistant went out on a limb for you," Danny said. "So don't go into one of your snits."

"Ooh, goody, rock shrimp." I hopped over a bowl of dip and perched on the shrimp dish. I began flicking the tiny shrimps into my mouth. "I don't go into snits," I said between mouthfuls. "At least, not without a good reason."

"You'd better not find any reason to louse this up," he warned.

"I won't louse it up," I promised. I scarfed down some more shrimp. "Why should I? I learned my lesson."

"Well, the only thing is . . ." He hesitated.

I stopped eating. "What only thing?"

"They've got a sort of . . . surprise I didn't tell you about."

"Surprise?" I sailed across the table and landed on a tray of cookies. "What do you mean, surprise?" I jumped off the tray and onto his knee. I stared up at him. "What are you pulling this time?"

"I'm not pulling anything!" he said. "It's not my show. Just, please, whatever happens—don't clam up."

"*Whatever happens?*" I cried. "What's going to happen?"

Jill stuck her head in the doorway. "Come on, kids. It's show time."

I sprang off Danny's knee and bounded across the room.

"Chan—Natasha!" he said. "Don't do this again!"

I huddled under the buffet table.

"Hop to it, Natasha," Jill said. "No need for nerves. Just be yourself."

"If I could be myself," I said, "I'd never go on your show."

Danny crawled under the table after me. "This could be our last chance," he said. "Don't blow it."

He was right. No matter what humiliating stunt they'd dreamed up, I couldn't throw a tantrum now.

"All right," I said finally. At least I'd had a hearty meal.

Jill led us to the edge of the set, where we could see the studio audience. Misty stood in a center aisle between two banks of seats.

"She says," Misty began, "his kiss turned her into a frog. He says their relationship just got off on the wrong foot. Welcome, please, Danny and Natasha."

The audience clapped as Danny carried me onstage. Misty pointed to a row of chairs, and Danny sat down. He put me on a chair next to him. I jumped as a microphone seemed to drop from the sky, and bobbed in front of me.

"I didn't tell our audience yet," Misty said, "the most amazing aspect of this relationship. Even though Natasha claims Danny turned her into a frog, she still has her powers of speech. That's right, Natasha can *talk!*"

The audience jeered and hooted, till Misty held up her

hand. "I know it's hard to believe," she said. "So I'll just let Natasha tell you herself." She turned to me. "Natasha, say hello to our audience."

"Hello to our audience," I said.

It sounded as if everyone in the studio gasped at once.

For a moment, there was silence. Then a few people started laughing at my silly joke. Others began to boo. Someone jeered.

"Wait a minute!" Misty scolded them. "Give Natasha a chance. Natasha, let's hear your story."

"There's not much to tell," I said nervously. "I was a normal teenage girl till he kissed me. Then, bam! The next thing I knew, I was a frog."

The audience grew quieter. A lot of them were leaning forward to see me better.

"That's so incredible," Misty said. "What would cause something like that to happen? Be straight with me, Natasha. Did you and Danny have a troubled relationship before you turned into a frog?"

"We didn't have any relationship at all," I said. "I hardly knew him."

"You hardly knew him," Misty said, "but you let him kiss you? Do you think that was a good idea?"

"Look at me!" I snapped. "Do *you* think it was a good idea?"

Most of the audience laughed, but a few were still shaking their heads. Some of the men made thumbs-down signs.

A girl with a mop of wild red hair and a nose ring stood up. Misty sprinted over to her and stuck a microphone in her face.

"How do we know she's really talking?" the girl demanded. "He could be a ventri—venquil—a guy who talks with a dummy."

"Ventriloquist," Misty said helpfully. "Danny, are you a ventriloquist?"

"No," I said. "He's the dummy." Good one, I thought.

The girl with the nose ring sat down as the audience clapped and whistled.

"Danny, why don't you tell us your side of the story? Why did you kiss Natasha in the first place?" Misty lowered her voice to a secretive whisper. "Did you have a secret crush on her?"

He looked uncomfortable. "It was just a—I mean—the thing was—"

"Oh, tell them the truth," I said. "Someone bet you a dollar you wouldn't kiss me."

Half the audience thought that was hilarious. The other half booed.

"But isn't this rather unusual?" Misty asked.

Rather unusual? What was the matter with this ditz?

"In the fairy tale," Misty explained, "a beautiful girl kisses the frog and he turns into a prince. Or Prince Charming kisses the frog and she turns into a princess."

"I guess he's my Prince Un-Charming," I said.

The audience laughed and clapped. They like me! I

thought. They really like me. I was turning out to be pretty good at this TV stuff.

"But we're not in a fairy tale," Danny said. "And we're not just trying to break into show business. We hoped that somebody watching your show might be able to help turn Ch—Natasha back into a human again."

"Speak for yourself, buster," I said. "I never got this much attention when I was human."

I was starting to enjoy the spotlight. And there was a certain giddy freedom in being a frog with a fake name and a snappy wit. The TV lights were hot, but so was I.

If I never turned back into a person, maybe I wouldn't have to go live in a swamp. Maybe I could launch a career in standup (or squat-down) comedy. "NATASHA! The world's first amphibian comedian!"

If nobody knew who I really was, I could be anyone I wanted.

"But seriously, folks," I said, "is there a zoologist in the house?"

"We don't have a zoologist with us," Misty said. "But we here at the *Misty Blake* show are always concerned with the welfare of our guests. So we have a special surprise for you."

Uh-oh.

"We've asked four of the hottest hunks in America to meet you," Misty said. "We're hoping that one of them will be your Prince Charming."

A short, curly-haired guy in a muscle shirt and bike

shorts swaggered onto the set. He had huge shoulders, a tiny waist, and no hips. He raised his arms and greeted the audience by rippling every visible muscle in his body.

The audience—at least, the women in the audience—shrieked and whistled.

"He's the star of the exercise video *From Flab to Fab,*" Misty announced. "Welcome, Jake Peck!"

I got chills. But not from Jake's pecs. This was the surprise Danny warned me about. I knew, with a terrible certainty, what Misty had planned.

Jake took a chair next to me. He shook Danny's hand and flexed a bulging bicep in my direction.

"Next," Misty went on, "from that famed Hollywood club Heppelwhite's, fabulous dancer Lance Harley!"

A tall, tanned, golden-haired gorgeous person strode onstage. The crowd went wild. Women screamed. My big frog eyes nearly popped out. Lance was wearing a stiff white collar and a black bow tie. No shirt, just the collar and tie. He had a very nifty chest. His black pants fit as snugly as a coat of paint.

He bowed gallantly and threw kisses to the audience. He sat down next to Jake.

"And now, the newest Hollywood heartthrob, star of the thrilling, chilling movie *Breakfast of Vampires,* Brad Stone!"

More screaming and whistling. I didn't think Brad Stone was any cuter than Danny.

"Finally," Misty said, "the romance-novel Romeo, whose classic face has been the model for hundreds of book covers. Ladies, don't faint on me—here's Sergio!"

Sergio was dressed like a pirate in a satin drawstring shirt, tight pants, maroon sash, and black leather boots. He wore a maroon bandanna over his shoulder-length black hair. One very large gold hoop dangled from one very large earlobe. He was carrying a red rose.

Good grief, I thought. What a getup.

Sergio looked out at the audience. He didn't smile. He just let his eyes smolder darkly at them. I thought Misty was going to have to get a whip and a chair to keep the crowd under control.

He turned, and approached my chair. He let his eyes smolder darkly at me. He held out the rose. "For you, Natasha," he said, with a slight accent.

"Thank you," I said. I looked down at the rose. There was an ant on one of the petals. My tongue flicked out and grabbed it.

"Eeuwww!" the audience groaned.

Sergio dropped the rose and quickly took a seat.

"We'll be right back after this break," Misty said, "to see if one of our hunks is the Prince Charming who will break Natasha's spell."

The cameras moved away and Misty huddled with the hunks. They were probably arguing over the pecking order. I couldn't hear what they were saying, but I assumed no one was fighting to go first.

I hopped onto Danny's shoulder. "This is the surprise, isn't it? These guys are going to kiss me."

"Yeah." Danny nodded. "It's kind of corny, but—"

"Corny?" I said. "It's humiliating."

"But you were willing to kiss any guy I could get the other day," Danny reminded me.

"Not on live TV," I said. "All of America is going to go 'eeuwww' when they see this."

"Ten seconds!" someone called out.

"You're making a public spectacle out of me," I said miserably.

"Just try not to puff up," Danny said.

You would think that being kissed by four guys who were supposed to be every woman's fantasy would be a thrilling experience.

You would be wrong.

A: None of them had ever figured in any of my fantasies.

B: I had never yearned to be kissed in front of a horde of hooting morons and an entire nation of couch potatoes.

And C: In none of my daydreams had I ever been a frog.

Misty hovered over us anxiously, holding out the microphone, as each man kissed me. I guess she wanted to capture my reaction if I miraculously turned back into a human.

She seemed crushed when the first three kisses produced no magic transformation.

Sergio went last. He made his eyes smolder at me again, which inflamed most of the women in the studio but only frightened me. With his face that close, his eyes seemed the size of bowling balls.

He planted his lips right on my mouth. I couldn't tell if the audience screamed because they were jealous or nauseated. He stepped back and folded his arms. He looked at me smugly, as if he were confident that no one could stay a frog after a kiss from Sergio.

"Do you feel anything, Natasha?" Misty asked.

"Not a thing," I said.

Sergio took back his rose.

Our segment of the show wound down after that. Danny gave out his phone number and asked anyone who might be able to help to get in touch with him.

The camera moved back from us. The red light went off.

"After this break," Misty announced: "He claims she treats their dog like a person. She claims he treats her like a dog! Don't go away!"

Jill hustled us off the stage.

"I guess I'm not going to be the world's first amphibian comedian," I said.

"What?" Danny asked.

"Never mind. Could we stop in the greenroom for a snack before we go home?"

TEN

When we got back to Danny's the phone was ringing and Bobo was howling. Danny tripped over the dog as he raced for the phone. I sprang from his hand as he fell, and landed on the answering machine before Bobo could step on me.

"Wow, we're a hit!" I said. "Fourteen messages!"

Danny untangled himself from Bobo but the phone stopped ringing before he could reach it. He started to play back the messages.

Two were from Mason Gorman. "Hey, where'd you get the frog?" and "Hey, how'd you do that?"

One was from an ad agency that wanted me to be the spokesfrog for Wild World Frog and Lizard Chow.

There was a long, angry message from the president of the Animal Rights Foundation. If Danny didn't stop exploiting me, A.R.F. would find a way to set me free in my natural environment. I shuddered.

A professor from the state university called to warn Danny that some frogs are poisonous, and people shouldn't be kissing me, even if the whole thing was just a stunt.

"He might be able to help." Danny wrote down the professor's number.

"Poisonous," I said indignantly. "*Moi?* I wouldn't hurt a fly."

"You *eat* flies," Danny reminded me.

"But I don't poison them."

I was pretty tired by this time and feeling kind of dry. "You'd better put me in the aquarium," I said.

"Shh." Danny was listening to the last message. I was too sleepy to pay attention. All I heard was ". . . just about finished here . . . ought to be home by . . ." Click. Whirr.

"The tape ran out!" Danny cried.

"So rewind it," I said. "After you put me in my aquarium."

"That was my dad. He's coming home, but I don't know when."

"Too bad." I didn't really care about anything right then except water and sleep. "Now, put me in the aquarium."

"Chandler, don't you get it? If my father—"

That was the last thing I heard as I fell asleep on the phone machine.

* * *

When I woke up I was in the aquarium. Danny was standing over me. His eyes were bleary, and his shoulders slumped. His mouth sagged, as if it took too much energy to keep it closed.

"You look like a zombie," I said.

"I feel like a zombie. The phone hasn't stopped ringing since yesterday."

"Wow, it's tomorrow already?" I hopped onto my rock. "I slept like a log."

"Lucky you," he said.

"Boy, I'm hungry." I jumped off the rock and took a few vigorous hops around the aquarium. "What's for breakfast? We should have taken home some of those little shrimps. We could have brought a doggy bag. Or a froggy bag. Ha! That's a good one. A froggy—"

"Chandler!" Danny rubbed his eyebrows. "Stop yammering."

"Was I yammering?" I dived into my water bowl. "That's odd. I don't usually yammer. I'm usually very quiet. Of course, I'm usually not a frog. Do you have any frozen shrimp? You could defrost them in the—"

"What's gotten into you?" he asked. "I've never seen you so hyper."

"I don't know. Maybe the tinsel and glitter of showbiz. I was pretty good on TV, wasn't I? Do you think I could really do commercials? Are there any anchovies left over from the pizza?"

"Chandler, we have to talk," he said. "I mean, I have to talk. You have to stop talking."

"What do we have to talk about? Did anyone call to say they could turn me back?"

"Half the world called," he said wearily. He picked up a yellow pad from his desk. "A neurosurgeon from the University Hospital wants to give you a CAT scan."

"You mean a frog scan," I said. "Ha ha. Why?"

"To see what makes you talk."

"We know what makes me talk," I said. "Cross him off the list. Who else?"

He looked down at the pad. "The Incredible Alistair."

"The magician? What did he want?"

"He wants you to be on his TV special."

"Wow! I *knew* I was good!"

"To prove you're a fraud," Danny finished.

"The jerk. Cross him off."

"And my aunt called."

"Uh-oh. Did she see us?"

"She sure did. And when my father called her she told him."

"Uh-oh."

"*Big* uh-oh," Danny agreed. "The only thing we have going for us is that I had the machine on when she called. So I didn't have to explain anything to her."

"Did she know when your father would be home?"

"He changed his flight," Danny said. "His plane comes into Kennedy at midnight tonight."

"What time is it now?" I asked.

"Nine-thirty. A.M."

"Then there's plenty of time."

"To do what?" Danny demanded.

"To get me something to *eat!*"

"Chandler, be reasonable. Can't you think of anything but food?"

"Not on an empty stomach," I said. "You might as well ask your dog to be reasonable when he's hungry."

"Okay, okay." He dashed out of the room and was back in a suspiciously short time with a dish of something. Whatever it is, he hadn't slaved over a hot stove preparing it.

He stuck the dish in the aquarium. "Noodles Alfredo," he said. "You'll like it. It should taste just like worms."

"You have a sarcastic streak yourself," I said between slurps of noodles. "It isn't very attractive."

The noodles were pretty good. I sucked them up with my tongue like strands of spaghetti, and they slid easily down my throat. It was kind of fun.

"I've been thinking," I began. "Would it really be so awful if *The Midnight Rambler* did a story on me?"

"Are you serious?" Danny looked stunned. "What about 'Frog Girl,' and putting bugs in your lunch, and being hounded for twenty years?"

"But I'm Natasha," I said. "And when I change back, Natasha will disappear. No one will ever know I was a frog."

He shook his head. "I think the tinsel and glitter have warped your brain. Listen. We might be able to get my father not to write your story. Or at least to hold it until you've changed back. But he's not our only problem."

"What do you mean?"

"Mason Gorman," Danny said. "I think he's figured it out."

I hissed. I could see my reflection in the aquarium glass. I was swelling up like I had a balloon under my chin. (If I had a chin.)

"Mason Gorman knows I turned into a frog?"

"He left a bunch of messages," Danny explained. "First he was joking about how he dared me to kiss you. Then he saw us on TV. I think he made the connection."

"Oh, no! How could we have been so stupid?"

"I don't know," Danny said. "I should have had them put a blue dot over me, or scramble my face, or something. It just never occurred to me that Mason would watch that show."

"It's a stupid show!" I snapped. "Of course he'd watch it!" I hopped nervously around the aquarium. "But how could he believe your kiss changed me into a frog? It's so fantastic."

Danny pointed to his yellow pad. "I have a list of forty-two people who also believed it. Plus Misty Blake and Jill and Snap Chapman's assistant and—"

"This is awful," I croaked. "If Mason knows, Jason knows. Which means everyone in school will know."

"Which means," Danny said, "that we'll never convince my father not to do a story on you, because you won't be a secret anymore."

"Which means I *will* be Frog Girl all my life, even after I change back. Agghhh!" I hopped frantically over my rock, through the potting soil, around the aquarium.

I practically hurled myself into the water bowl.

"I might as well stay a frog!" I screamed. "My life is over!"

"I have a plan," Danny said quietly.

I stuck my head out of the water and peered at him. "You do? Well, why didn't you say so? What's the plan?"

"It's not exactly a plan," he said. "Just sort of a holding action. We need to buy a little time."

"Plan, holding action, who cares?" I said. "Cut to the chase."

"There's no one home at your house, right?"

"That's right," I said. "Horace is in Switzerland, and Mrs. Gruen has till next Monday off."

"We hide out there," Danny said. "No one will find us, and maybe you'll change back by Monday."

"What good will hiding out do?" I asked. "Mason already knows about me."

"He's just guessing, so far," Danny said. "And if you change back before he sees you, who's going to believe him?"

"But what about you?" I asked. "You can't just disappear. Your father will go nuts. And what if someone calls who can change me back, and we're not here to—"

"I've got it all figured out," Danny began. "I can get the messages from another—"

The doorbell rang. Bobo began to bark.

"Don't answer it!" I said. "What if it's Mason?"

"Don't worry. I'll look through the peephole before I open up."

I heard the sound of the door opening and closing, and then a woman's voice speaking in low, rapid tones.

I heard the door slam. Danny raced into the room. He pulled his backpack out of the closet and started throwing things in it wildly. "We've got to get out of here!"

"What is it?" I asked. "What's wrong?"

"That was Mrs. Forbush. She lives downstairs." He yanked a hooded sweatshirt over his head. He snatched me out of the aquarium and shoved me into the pocket of the backpack.

"Hey! Not so rough!" I protested.

"Stay in there and shut up," he ordered. "Don't say a word till we're out of this building."

"Why? What's going on?"

"Two men were just asking Mrs. Forbush all sorts of questions about me." He slung the pack over his shoulder so I couldn't see his face.

"She didn't know what they wanted," he said. "All she knew was that they were from the CIA."

ELEVEN

Danny stopped his bike halfway up the circular driveway.

"This is your house?"

"I guess it is," I said. "I can only see behind us, you know."

"Wow! It looks like a castle."

He pulled me from the backpack and I jumped onto his shoulder.

"I don't suppose you have a key on you?" he asked.

"Gee, no," I said. "I must have left it in my other body. But there's one in the pool house." I jumped to the ground. "Come on."

I led him past the garages to the patio area.

"Wow!"

"Haven't you ever seen a pool before?" I said irritably.

"Not like this one."

"It is pretty, I guess," I admitted. There was a large

bluestone patio with white lawn furniture. A short flight of stone steps led down to the free-form, Olympic-size pool. White screens and masses of plantings made it look like the tropics.

"You could have great parties here," Danny said.

"Yeah. I'll invite all my frog friends."

The pool house was a white latticework octagon with louvered doors. The house key was under a pile of floats. Danny pulled it out and we went into the house through the service entrance off the kitchen. I told Danny the security code, and he punched it in to deactivate the alarm system.

"Okay," I said. "We're here, no one can find us. Now will you please tell me what in the world the CIA wants with you?"

"Not me," he said. "You."

"What could they want with me?"

"Don't you see?" he said. "You'd be the perfect spy."

"Me? A *spy?*" I started to laugh. "That's ridiculous! Where would I keep my secret code book? Where would I find a trench coat to fit me? How would I—"

"Didn't you ever see *Day of the Dolphin?*" he said. "Chandler, it's no joke."

"Who would I spy on?" I couldn't stop laughing. "Terrorist frogs?"

"Fine," he snapped. "It's hilarious. But I'm just trying to protect you."

"Well, the CIA can't find me here," I said. "What I'm

really worried about is Mason. How are you going to protect me from him?"

"I never actually talked to him," Danny said. "The machine took all his calls. I'm hoping he won't tell anyone till he knows for sure."

"That's pretty weak," I said. "I don't think Mason would worry about spreading nasty rumors."

The phone rang, startling me so that I jumped halfway down the back hall. It stopped after one and a half rings.

"The answering machine must be on," I said.

"Where is it?"

"In the library. This way." I hopped along the back hall to the entry foyer.

"Wow!" he marveled. "This is bigger than my whole apartment."

"Come on." I led him into the library, just in time to hear the beep signaling the end of the message.

"It's dark in here," Danny said.

"The curtains are closed," I said. "Switch on the lamp." I jumped onto the desk and looked at the green light on the answering machine. "Five messages. I wonder who called."

Danny lit the banker's lamp on the desk. He pressed the "New Messages" button, and the machine started playing back the calls.

"Chan, it's Lauren. I wanted to say good-bye before I left for Florida. Call me if you get in before tomorrow. Bye."

"Hi, Chandler, it's Kelly. Where'd you go? What happened with Danny? Call me before you go to camp. I'll be here till Sunday. Bye."

There were two more messages from Lauren. Her voice sounded more anxious in each one.

"She sure seems upset," Danny said. "I hope she doesn't think I did something to you."

I stared at him. "Why would anyone think that?"

"Don't be sarcastic," he said. "I meant, something bad."

"Turning me into a frog was a *good* thing?"

The last message was from Teen Wilderness Adventures. They wanted to know why I hadn't shown up for survival camp, and to remind Horace that half the fee was nonrefundable.

I sighed. "Survival camp would have been a piece of cake compared to this. I can't believe I was worried about a silly little thing like falling down a mountain."

Danny reached into his pocket and pulled out the list of people who had phoned about me. "I'm going to start calling some of these people," he said. "There's a biologist in a lab at—"

"No labs! I'm not going anyplace where they dissect stuff."

"Do you think I'd let anybody dissect you?" He reached for the phone.

Bong! Bong!

I jumped again. I'd gotten so used to the sounds of Danny's place that I'd forgotten the sounds of my own.

Bong, bong, *bong*.

"Do you have a grandfather clock?" Danny asked.

"That's the doorbell," I whispered. At least, I tried to whisper.

"Who could it be?"

"How should I know?" I answered.

"Can you see the front door from the windows in here?" he asked.

"No, but you can see part of the driveway."

"Maybe it's just a UPS delivery, or something like that." He went to the windows and pushed the curtain aside slightly.

"Don't let them see you!" I warned. "Is it UPS?"

He dropped the curtain. When he turned back toward me his eyes were huge.

"What's the matter?" I asked. "Who's out there?"

Bong! Bong!

"The army," he said. His knees buckled and he slid to the floor.

"Don't faint again!" I forgot to whisper, but it didn't matter. The army was shouting and pounding on the door so hard they couldn't have heard me.

"Open up! We know you're in there! We have this area secured!"

Danny's eyes were open, but glazed, like he was only partly conscious.

"What do you think our chances are of not making the six o'clock news?" I asked.

"I only saw two jeeps," he said weakly. "And a limo. Maybe none of the neighbors noticed. Lots of land between houses here."

"Open up in the name of national security!"

"How did they find us?" I wondered.

Danny just shook his head.

"We are authorized to force entry!"

"I don't suppose they're bluffing," I said hopefully.

Another voice, loud enough to hear, but calmer. "Danny, we just want to talk to you. We think we might be able to help you. Please let us in."

"You might as well," I said. "They're not going to go away."

Danny got slowly to his feet. "Find a place to hide," he said. "And don't come out."

"What about you?"

"It's not me they want." He started toward the foyer. "Go on," he urged. "*Hide.* And no matter what happens, *don't talk.*"

It was a big house, and there were plenty of places to hide, but I wanted to be able to hear what was going on. I looked around the library.

"Hurry up!" Danny said. Then, louder, "I'm coming, I'm coming! Just a minute!"

I spotted a large brass urn near the door to the library. In three bounds I reached it and jumped inside. It was full of marble chips. I burrowed down into them till only my eyes were exposed.

I heard the front door open.

"Danny Malone?" a voice asked.

"What do you want?" Danny asked.

"My name is Richard Arbuckle. This is General Manton of the Military Intelligence Council. And Dr. Jeanette Hess from the National Institute of Science."

"Can I see some ID?" Danny asked.

"Of course," said Mr. Arbuckle. "That's very sensible."

"How did you find me?"

"We followed you," a gruff voice answered.

"We just want to talk to you." A woman's voice this time. "May we come in and sit down? We'll all be more comfortable."

"I'm not comfortable when two guys with rifles are standing over me," Danny said.

"Wait outside," the gruff voice ordered. I heard the door close.

"This is quite a house," Mr. Arbuckle said pleasantly. I heard footsteps moving away. Danny was taking them into the living room. "Whose is it?" Mr. Arbuckle asked. "I know it's not yours."

"Am I under arrest?" Danny demanded.

"Of course not!" Mr. Arbuckle chuckled.

"Then I don't have to answer any questions," Danny said. "And I'm not going to."

"If you'll let us explain why we need your help, I'm sure you'll want to cooperate," Mr. Arbuckle said. "Any patriotic citizen would."

"Cooperate how?" asked Danny.

"It's come to our attention," the gruff voice said, "that you may be in possession of an intelligent frog."

"I'm not," Danny lied.

"Danny, we have the tape of the television show you did," Mr. Arbuckle said. "Shall I play it for you?"

"It's a fake," Danny said quickly. "The frog can't really talk."

"It certainly seemed to be talking," Dr. Hess said.

"That was me," Danny said.

"You're a ventriloquist?" asked Dr. Hess.

"Yeah. That's all it was. I just wanted to get on TV."

"How interesting." Dr. Hess sounded deceptively sweet. "Would you show me how you did the frog's voice?"

"I can't," Danny said. "A ventriloquist never reveals his secrets."

"That's a magician," Mr. Arbuckle said. "A ventriloquist doesn't have any secrets."

"Then you should already know how I ventrocle—ventrilo—do the voice," Danny said.

I huddled in the urn, shivering. Not because I was buried in marble chips. Danny was a poor liar. I was sure that this casual interview would soon turn into a nasty confrontation.

It didn't take long.

"Where's the frog, Danny?" Mr. Arbuckle wasn't chuckling anymore.

"I let it loose," Danny said. "In Central Park. After we did the show."

"Don't play games with us, Malone," the gruff voice said. "This is a matter of national security."

"General, please, let me," Dr. Hess said. "Danny, we're not going to hurt your frog. We just need to study it, so we can find the mechanism responsible for speech."

"Why?"

"For science," she said. "If we can find out how the frog talks, we might be able to create other animals that can communicate with man."

"But if it's purely for science," Danny said, "what's the CIA and the army doing here?"

"Well . . ." She hesitated. "Of course there may be some military applications—"

"We're not prepared to discuss that at the present," Mr. Arbuckle cut in.

"I knew it!" Danny said. "It's *Day of the Dolphin* all over again!"

"We've danced around long enough!" the general barked. "I want that frog and I want it now."

I heard the front door open, then heavy boots tramping in the foyer. "Frog!" the general shouted. "Small! Green! Find it!"

"Yes, sir!" two voices answered.

"Wait!" Danny shouted. "You can't just barge in here like this!"

"We didn't barge in," Mr. Arbuckle said. "You let us in." He didn't sound the least bit pleasant now. "We tried to do this the friendly way," he went on. "But we're getting nowhere. I'll have to ask you to come with us."

I nearly screamed. I popped my head above the urn and tried to see into the foyer.

"What do you mean?" Danny asked. His voice shook. "Come with you where?"

"To Washington," Arbuckle said. "Maybe you'll feel more like cooperating there."

"You can't do that!" Danny protested. "That's kidnapping!"

"This is a matter of gravest national importance," the general said. "Soldiers, escort him to—"

"No!" I screamed. "Leave him alone!"

I scrambled up through the marble chips and out of the urn. I bounded into the entry hall.

They all turned to look at me. Three men in uniform, and a woman. And one man in a brown suit—and, yes, a trench coat.

"You don't need him," I said. "It's me you want."

The general gasped. The two soldiers dropped their jaws and lifted their rifles.

"Don't shoot!" I cried. I hopped behind Danny's legs.

Dr. Hess bent down to take a closer look at me. "It's true," she breathed. She straightened up. "Put those guns away!"

Only Mr. Arbuckle seemed unexcited.

"You'll come with us," he said to me, "of your own free will?"

"Don't Chan!" Danny pleaded. "We don't know what they're going to do to you."

My whole body began to tremble, as if little waves were rippling under my skin. It must be a fear reaction, I thought. Like puffing up.

Because I was scared. Danny was right. I had no idea what they were planning to do to me. I didn't really think they'd enlist me as a spy, but labs and scientists and experiments were probably in my future.

They might even try to clone me. I wondered if it would hurt.

I felt an oozing sensation, as if my skin were turning liquid. It was so weird. Like nothing I'd ever felt before, either human or frog.

"I'll go." I rubbed one of my stubby front legs against the side of my head. "But you can't take Danny."

If I told them the whole story, if they realized that I hadn't started out as a frog, but as a person, maybe they'd lose interest. I wasn't really a talking animal, after all. I was just a green human.

"What is it doing?" General Manton asked suddenly.

My skin started to itch. It was wet and icky. What was happening to me? I tugged at my skin and felt something peeling, as if I were stripping off a surgical glove. I scraped and pulled, as much as I could reach with my short legs.

"She's shedding her skin." Danny and Dr. Hess said it together.

Now I was dragging the stuff over my head. I remembered what Danny said I did with the old skin.

No way! I wasn't going to eat this! I just wanted to get rid of it. It was covering my eyes now. I couldn't see anything. Not the boots, not Dr. Hess's suede loafers, not Mr. Arbuckle's trench coat. I couldn't see the rifles, or Danny's frantic eyes.

My tongue flicked out, as instinctively as it flicked to catch bugs. With it I drew the skin away from my eyes.

I felt a sudden whoosh of air, as if I were zooming upward in a drafty elevator. I yanked the last bits of skin off my face.

When my vision cleared, I was looking right into Danny's eyes.

"Chandler! You're back!" He whooped, and threw his arms around me. I screamed for joy, and threw my arms around him. He lifted me off my feet and swung me around.

We jumped around the foyer, crying and yelling and holding on to each other.

General Manton fainted.

TWELVE

That afternoon I ate my first meal in a week as a human. Rock lobster tails and sirloin steak. Danny broiled the steak, and I followed the directions on the freezer package for cooking the lobster tails.

"Isn't this delicious?" I sighed.

"Sure beats microwave chili," he said.

"And moths." He was watching me so intently as I ate that I began to feel self-conscious. "Why are you staring at me like that?"

"It's nice to see you eat with a fork instead of your tongue," he said.

I blushed.

"I'm going to miss taking care of you," he added.

"Really?" I felt myself turn redder. But it hardly bothered me. "I thought I was a lot of trouble."

"You were," he said. "But it was exciting, too."

"I'm exciting?" No one had ever thought I was exciting before.

"As a frog you were" he said. "I don't know you as a human. But you were a very interesting amphibian."

The phone rang.

"Where have you *been?*" Kelly demanded. "I just got back from my father's *this minute,* and I was frantic about you the whole time I was there. I mean, I couldn't even concentrate on my tan, I was so . . ."

Lauren called last night. "Why did you just go off like that, without saying anything? I thought you might be mad at me, but I couldn't figure out what I'd done. I was so worried I accidentally ate a burrito with beef in it."

"I'm sorry," I told her. "I wasn't mad at you."

"Then what happened? Did you go to survival camp?"

"Well . . . sort of."

"Are you going to tell them?" Danny asked, when I hung up.

"I don't know," I said. "I have a lot of things to think about."

Oddly enough, it was Danny's father who guided me through the legal maze of getting Horace undeclared my guardian. And he didn't even pressure me to do an interview for *The Midnight Rambler.*

"You're not a talking frog anymore," he told me. "So there's no story."

"But all those people saw me on television," I reminded him. "Even though they didn't know it was me."

"You were famous for five minutes," he said. "Stay off TV for a week and someone else will become famous."

He found a custody lawyer, who brought in an accountant to examine the expenses Horace claimed he'd paid out for my benefit.

They convinced a surrogate court judge that my cousin had spent a whole lot of my inheritance on things that benefited him, not me.

I became a "ward of the state," which sounds awful but isn't. I got to hire the person who will live with me until I start college.

Her name is Liz Tortola. She's studying for her Ph.D. at the state university. We swim every day. Liz taught me. She couldn't believe how quickly I took to the water.

"It's like you really wanted to all along," she said, "but were just afraid to let yourself go."

Mr. Arbuckle calls every once in a while to find out if I've changed back into a frog. For a time I tried to convince him that he and Dr. Hess and the army had imagined the whole thing.

"Mass hypnosis," I told him. "You were all victims of a delusion. Have you thought about seeing a psychiatrist?"

Now whenever he calls, I just say, "ribbit" and hang up the phone.

Danny told Mason that the *Misty Blake* show was a

scam. He said he'd gotten the idea from a *Teach Yourself Ventriloquism* video. He told him I'd never even let him kiss me in the first place.

I'm not sure Mason believed the story. But he did demand his dollar back. And soon—just as Danny's father predicted—he stopped talking about it altogether.

A week after I changed back, I invited Lauren and Kelly for a sleepover.

They didn't even bring their swimsuits.

"Tell," they insisted. "We're your friends. We have a right to know."

I looked down at my hands. "Danny kissed me."

Kelly screamed and pretended to faint.

"Okay," Lauren said calmly, as if she wasn't a bit surprised. "Then what happened?"

You have to trust *someone,* I told myself. You have to trust your friends.

I took a deep breath. "It's a long story . . ."